IN THE NAME OF LOVE

"Aren't you going to invite me in, Edith?" John snapped as he walked through the door and locked it behind him.

It was hard to believe they had once been lovers because Edith now felt nothing but loathing and disgust. She didn't think he would hurt her until she suddenly remembered the time he raped her—how she had fought him, and how he had won.

Edith smiled and tried to keep John talking, knowing it was the only way to calm him—but it didn't work.

"Why did you betray me, you whore?" he screamed as he rushed toward her and pulled her hair viciously back. It hurt and she tried to remove his hand from her head. But he grabbed it tighter. It was his way of trying to seduce and bully her at the same time.

"I want you to get rid of that guy you're with and come with me. See what I have here?"

He pulled a gun out of the inside of his jacket pocket.

"It's real, it works, and I use it when I need to . . ."

Edith panicked, because she knew the power of his emotions. She knew that once John was angered, there was no stopping him . . .

FRIENDS

BY ELIEBA LEVINE

ZEBRA BOOKS
KENSINGTON PUBLISHING CORP.

ZEBRA BOOKS

are published by

KENSINGTON PUBLISHING CORP.
21 East 40th Street
New York, N.Y. 10016

Printed in the United States of America

Dear Edith,

How fun to read your letter. To think of you in Paris! Here there's been a ninety-five-degree heat spell, and Paul and I just spent another regressive weekend. I can't plan with him, either to go away or to get a summer place. Besides, Nicholas called and told me he'd be in New York soon. It's gotten me all fucked up again and now Paul isn't talking to me because we've been living at such a low level.

Today we went to Jones Beach and I saw a woman playing in the water with her two children and the sight of her made my heart go out. Paul was furious that after all these weeks of work that's all he gets—a trip to Jones Beach in my brother's old, sputtering Volkswagen. I've somehow managed to accept the lousiness of the situation.

I'm still working and the most ironic part is that the editor of the film turns out to be another of those MAGIC MEN I'd like to be rid of. He's married, has a six-year-old daughter, and, for the past two years, has lived on a farm with his wife. David Marin is totally attractive, like a warm James Caan with a beard. Resembles Nicholas, too. Has Paul's sanity. The wife is difficult and very suspicious; he never has affairs, he said. Here's a good chance for me to learn to establish a friendship—not rely on sexual attractions for approval, but on work and general good spirits. Oy! It's difficult to be an assistant. But then it's also difficult to take on the responsibility to cut that film. It would be better to smoke.

I liked Pascale; we spent a pleasant evening on my birthday. Paul was working. It seems you're in good hands. *These* French people seem to be the ones with life in them. I love the idea of you with them.

I feel good about making $309 a week, even if it is difficult to be David's assistant. At least that's real. More real than the MAGIC MEN I'm attracted to, who are also the men that make me fear myself. I think it's about time I got off this dead-end street that leads to nothing but trouble.

Otherwise, Paul is doing very well. Everyone is out to get him to shoot a film for them. He's becoming very successful, as we knew he would.

As for me, I'm just beginning to wonder about this incredible tramp that seems to live inside me. That's harsh, but I see how incredibly unfaithful I am. Because I never learned to establish a deep bond or understanding with anyone, I can't seem to work to hold on to anything. That worries me.

HOW ARE YOU?????????

Hope all is going well.
Regards to Pascale.

Love you,
Sarah

Edith put down the letter. At this moment Edith missed Sarah, missed New York. She looked out the window. The rooftops of Paris looked ancient.

When Edith skipped from the fourth to the sixth grade, she immediately knew Sarah was the one girl in class to be her friend. That took some doing, as it meant breaking an alliance between Sarah and her B.F., in those days short for *best friend.* A strategy had to be mapped out. Would Sarah respond if Edith played on her pity? She decided to try it. If that didn't work there were always other manipulations.

Edith (age ten) to herself: "I'll give her the soulful look next time we play jump rope."

It worked. Even in those days Sarah was a sucker for sadness. Edith dissolved Sarah's previous friendship, tactfully pointing out that Sarah was too smart for her old friend. Also, Edith continued, rumor had it that the friend's father was a gangster. Sarah listened and agreed. Soon the two exchanged friendship rings. Edith followed by beating up the class bully, which put her over the top.

Sarah was always popular. Had she not been, Edith probably would never have singled her out. Edith had a good eye for people and knew how to achieve her own ends. If she had so little trouble winning over a class of ten-year-old strangers in four weeks, why not the world in forty years?

By the time Edith and Sarah were fourteen and entering high school, they were inseparable. Physically, Edith was fully grown and fully blossomed, while Sarah was still putting stockings in her bra. They both had green eyes and thick brown hair, but Sarah's face was long like her mother's, while Edith's was round like her father's. For all their similarities, Edith was considered the greater beauty of the two. Sarah never understood this and spent much time scrutinizing Edith's face. Was it her fairer complexion or smaller nose? Why was Edith so adored for her face? It affected Edith, too. There were times when she needed to gaze at herself to know she was alive. If Edith's mother caught her stopping at a mirror, she raged at the child unmercifully. Edith didn't understand. The two people she loved most were angered by her beauty. She often wondered what it was that people considered so rare in her face. From the time she was twelve, men followed her home and tried to entice her into their cars, a situation that threw her into confused feelings of pleasure and rage. And so, at times, each girl wished it were possible to change places with the other.

One afternoon after school, the two girls sat in the indoor porch of Edith's house in Brooklyn. It was built of red brick and was attached to another one just like it. In the front was a lawn which ran the length of both houses, bushes planted close to the houses for decoration. It was a typical middle-class house in a typical middle-class Jewish neighborhood. It was Brooklyn. The porch where Edith and Sarah sat was covered with floral wallpaper and furnished simply. A rocking chair sat ignored in a corner. Edith sat on the couch and Sarah in one of the armchairs as they spoke, playing catch with a Spaulding rubber ball. Edith listened to Sarah.

"I just can't stand being in my house. My mother seems to have no control over herself. She walks around crying all the time and then apologizes. The other day she almost drove the car into a truck." Edith raised her arm to throw the ball and held it there as she spoke. "What could be wrong with her?" She released the ball.

"I don't know but I'd like to stay here for a few days if it's all right with your mother."

"I don't understand you, Sarah. Aren't you afraid to be away from home with your mother acting so strange?"

"What's there to be afraid of?"

"I'm not sure, but when I don't see my mother or

know where she is, I always think she's dead."

"Well, my mother isn't dying. It's probably her change of life. You really get scared about your mother?"

"Yes. . . ." They continued their game of catch in silence.

Edith lay in her bed. Sarah was asleep beside her. Edith had asked and been given permission for Sarah to spend a few days with them. They explained that Sarah's mother wasn't feeling well. Even if Edith's mother objected, with illness as an excuse she couldn't say no. Each time Sarah moved, Edith picked up her head hoping to find her friend awake. She wanted to speak of her fears. She was sure she heard babies crying in the houses next door and was convinced that her neighbors were kidnappers. Tonight in bed flashes of light crossed her eyes. They must be bringing in some new babies, she thought.

As these thoughts floated through her head, she finally fell asleep. With sleep came dreams. Dreams of being Wonder Woman and soaring high in the sky. Instead of a cape Edith had big green wings. Her ecstatic flight became troubled. An equally powerful woman was flying toward her with a hideous grin on her face. Blood poured out from between her teeth and she held a knife in one of her hands. Edith noticed those hands very well. They were much too large for a woman's and Edith flew faster, higher. The woman pursued her, blood dripping from her gums the whole time. Edith jumped up. She looked around. Sarah still slept. Edith knew she had been dreaming but closed her eyes just the same. If she dared open them that woman might be standing in her room, at her door, anywhere. Her eyes stayed shut so that she might not see a figure in the dark, but she also knew that sleep might bring her back. So Edith spent this night like so many others, awake for half of it with her eyes tightly closed.

***

"My parents want to know if we'd like to see a show with them tomorrow night. My mother probably feels guilty." The girls were having their usual game of catch on the porch.

"What show?"

"Mother told me but I forget."

Edith nodded her head.

Sarah's parents picked up the girls at Edith's house. Edith liked going places with them. They looked so elegant seated in their shiny black Cadillac. Mrs. Sherman always wore large black hats with velvet or feathered trimmings. Her hair was pulled tight back in a bun which accentuated her long face and large cocoa-colored eyes. Her lipstick just missed her top lipline and went over it, giving the slightest impression of smudged lips.

Edith always found this very attractive, especially compared to her own mother, who wore no lipstick at all.

As Edith entered the backseat of the car with Sarah, she noticed Mrs. Sherman's shoes—high-heeled black suede with ankle straps. Her own mother wore corrective shoes, stressing the importance of good feet. Though Edith's mother was considered a great beauty, Edith loved glamour more. To her, glamour was beauty.

Mr. Sherman was as elegant as his wife. He was adored by all women, including his daughter, for his good looks and easy charm.

The car made its way to the city. Sarah's parents, deep in discussion, paid little attention to the girls in the backseat. Edith's roving eyes noticed that Mrs. Sherman kept twisting and untwisting a handkerchief around her thumb as she spoke. Soon she was weeping. Edith tried to hear their conversation, but Sarah would not keep quiet long enough for her to understand their discussion. The strange thing about the ride was that Sarah didn't seem to notice her mother's anxiety or pain. Sarah would not be silenced.

Sarah went home with her parents that night. Edith got into bed and thought about Sarah's mother. She could vividly see her high-heeled shoes and quiet tears. She began rubbing her thighs together hoping for pleasure. As she did, an image of beautiful dresses came before her. The dresses were familiar . . . they belonged to one of her counselors at camp. Edith had loved her because of those dresses. She had wanted them desperately and thought about stealing them, but never could. Continuing to rub her thighs, she felt a surge of pleasure in her groin as she fantasized about having men steal for her. She saw herself directing a robbery. It would be a robbery of beautiful possessions.

Edith closed her eyes and imagined herself walking through a park. Two men are running and she runs after them. They see her and stop. The three of them stand like statues confronting one another. No one speaks. Edith places herself between them and they leave the park together. They walk through the streets. Suddenly she stops them at a beautiful boutique. They still do not speak but enter the store. One of them takes out a gun while the other casually opens the cash register and removes the money. While they are occupied, Edith fills bag after bag with the clothes she's longed for. They leave the store and walk to her house. The two faceless men and Edith instinctively enter her bedroom. Still, no one speaks. Edith throws her new possessions on the floor and proceeds to undress. She then gets into bed and covers herself with a sheet. They watch her and also undress. Both men approach her, pull down the sheet, and lie on either side of her. The room is dark, but just enough of the moon comes in through the windows to cast light on their naked bodies. Edith props her head up the slightest bit and stares at the two men. She looks from one to the other and suddenly bends over to kiss the older and darker of the two. He stirs while lifting his hand to stroke her hair. The room they are in changes from her bedroom to an old, elegant boudoir. Satin drapes the color of salmon are held against the windows by thick braided tiebacks. Small satin French chairs to match the drapes, and a curving chaise longue are set in the corner of the room, as if put there as an afterthought. Their kissing stops long enough for her to look at the room. She thinks of the people who might have stayed in this room before her—kings and their mistresses perhaps. The room and bed feel that way: lusty, decadent, once peopled by kings, queens, and secret lovers. "I am a whore now, but soon I will be a queen," With those words, her release was complete and Edith fell asleep.

Sarah and Edith, Edith and Sarah. It didn't matter which name was mentioned first. Whenever people talked about one of them, invariably they would also speak of the other. That's because Sarah and Edith were still friends after thirty years.

They were 38 now. Sarah's mother had committed suicide and Sarah was married to Paul, who was ten years her junior. He was a Methodist minister's son raised in Ohio. He had come to New York to make films. Paul was a cameraman, Sarah a film editor. They had met working on a low-budget documentary together. Sarah married Paul because in truth she had just about run out of options. The artist she'd been living with no longer desired her and work had been hard to find. At thirty, she was getting on in age and her Indian guru said she should learn how to share, as one would have to in a marriage. A month after meeting Paul, she married him. She had considered their relationship so commonplace that she never mentioned him to Edith until she announced one day that she was getting married. Edith's questions came in a rush of surprise.

"Who is he, where did he come from, what does he do, and, of course, when will I meet him?"

"His name is Paul Naughton, he's from Ohio, he's only twenty years old, wants to direct films some day, and I guess you'll meet him at our wedding. It's next week. Don't be shocked when you see him, he and his family are very WASP. That's the only thing that really troubles me. They're all so pale and white, not at all familiar looking."

Edith's voice registered confusion. "Weren't you telling me a few days ago how much you liked some black dude in your encounter group?"

Sarah's first sexual experience had been with a Haitian. Ever since then she'd always preferred dark men. "I guess I'm getting a little tired and frightened. Paul is kind and says he loves me."

"Won't it be a little like marrying your younger brother?"

"Maybe."

"I think you like being unconventional. Where

are you getting married?"

"In a friend's loft."

Edith smiled and ran her fingers through her dark brown hair.

That had been eight years ago.

Now Sarah and Edith were sitting in the booth of a restaurant about to have lunch. It was an elegant place, the walls and ceiling done in mirrors. It was impossible not to see yourself from almost any angle desired. Since Sarah and Paul lived downtown, the two women didn't see much of each other. They spoke every day on the phone, but it wasn't quite the same; they enjoyed looking at one another. On this day Sarah was wearing a dark green, threadbare looking suit and laced up boots. She looks like a stylized waif, Edith thought. Edith self-consciously looked at her own French jeans, her cowboy boots—which had cost a small fortune—and her nubbly beige sweater. Sarah spoke first.

"I've been getting these really dirty phone calls. I'm sure it's Nicholas."

Edith looked at her. "How can you be sure?"

"He says personal things that only Nicholas would know."

"Then why is he pretending to be someone else?"

Sarah, thinking, answered slowly. "I think it's his way of making contact."

Edith shrugged. "Doesn't sound right to me. You both know you'd never hang up on him if he identified himself. In fact, your conversation would probably get dirtier."

Sarah seemed not to hear Edith and went on talking. "You know, he keeps identifying himself as Tony, and he asked me to meet him in front of Klein's on Fourteenth Street. I played along with him and asked how I'd recognize him. He said not to worry, he'd recognize me. He then suggested I wear a maid's uniform, apron and all."

The waiter approached the table. Edith motioned him away. She looked straight into Sarah's eyes as she spoke.

"Don't tell me you actually did it."

Sarah nodded her head. "I stood there in the maid's uniform for over an hour. No one came. I was freezing. *Charmant, n'est pas?*"

"Didn't you feel humiliated?"

Sarah spoke without emotion. "With Nicholas, nothing is humiliating."

The waiter approached the table again. Sarah ordered her usual plain salad and coffee; Edith ordered a hamburger and Coke. They were quiet for a while, then Edith spoke. Her tone was patronizing.

"Remember the time Nicholas gave you that black eye and threw your cactus plant out the window? You actually seemed proud, almost as if it were the greatest display of love."

Sarah answered simply.

"I did feel proud. It reminded me of when I was a little girl and my father hit my sister and not me. I always thought he loved her more. When Nicholas hit me, I was finally the favorite."

For a few moments they lost themselves in eating.

"You could have left Paul and gone with Nicholas. He wanted to marry you."

"I can't leave Paul."

Edith suddenly hated Sarah's passivity and could almost understand Nicholas giving her that black eye. There was nothing more to say. They left the mirrored restaurant and parted on the street. Their usual friendly kiss good-bye was forced. "I'm glad to be away from her," thought Edith, as she hailed a passing taxi.

Edith opened her front door just in time to answer her ringing telephone. It was Sarah.

"How did you get home so fast?"

"The subway is a lot faster than a taxi, Edith."

Edith began pacing back and forth with the phone. "Anything earth shattering happen since lunch?"

"That Tony character called again and this time I wasn't sure it was Nicholas."

"What made you change your mind?"

"His voice; it was different. He said he was stoned."

"Sarah, I suggest if he calls again, threaten him with the police, hang up, do anything, but don't talk to him."

"But what if it is Nicholas?"

Edith grimaced. "Sarah, I just walked into the house. I'll call you later." She banged down the phone and began to undress.

Whenever she came home she automatically got undressed and slipped into a robe. Edith carefully hung up her jeans to make sure they didn't crease. Her boots were placed on the floor of the closet.

She looked down at them and smiled. "My feet look like they're still in them," she thought. She folded her sweater neatly and put it in her armoire. With a sigh of relief she sat down on the edge of her bed and surveyed her room.

All her jewelry was displayed on her double dresser. It consisted of long silver necklaces from Africa, beads hanging from silver or gold chains, bracelets made of silver and ivory, and a large gold locket given to her by her mother. Her mirror hung above the dresser and was draped on either side with a variety of colored scarves. She kept these objects within sight because she enjoyed looking at them. There were two small night tables on either side of the bed. They were low, with wood bases and marble tops. Piles of papers and periodicals completely covered the marble. Her bed was large and low to the floor. The room faced south, allowing the sunlight to invade her large bay window. This was Edith's favorite room.

The rest of the apartment she thought rather ordinary. It consisted of a small kitchen and good sized living room. Outside of a desk and couch, she had no real furniture to speak of. Oversized pillows and a low coffee table, and that was it.

Edith was a writer. As yet she made little money for her efforts, but she was fortunate enough to receive a small income from her family which sustained her. She wrote scripts, stories, and books. Sometimes she agonized over her writing and preferred to vacuum her apartment or clean the closets rather than face her typewriter. In truth it was really quite simple. Edith was happier when she was writing than when she wasn't, and that was that. Her excuse for occasional depravity, insincerity with men, loveless sex, was that it was all in the name of research. The truth is that Edith was afraid of her imagination. When she was small her neighbors were kidnappers. Now, certain dark men on the street carried knives and wanted to kill her. This anxiety would pass when she was with her present lover, John. He was a powerful businessman, who also was handsome, rich, and not lacking in humor.

"I'm glad I have John," thought Edith as she got up from her bed and looked out her window, staring aimlessly. "At least he's not insane like Sarah's lover seems to be. Sarah and her MAGIC MEN." Edith smiled to herself and walked away from the window.

***

John looked at himself in his bathroom mirror. He touched a spot of blood on his chin. "Damn it. Why can't I ever shave without cutting myself?" He splashed on some cold water to wash away the evidence of his self-inflicted wound. He was trying to ready himself to meet Edith at their usual restaurant. He stared down at his watch which rested on the side of the sink. "I've plenty of time." He returned his gaze to the mirror and smiled at himself.

Life had changed since mutual friends had introduced him to Edith. He felt freer, less constrained. He didn't even care if he were five minutes late for an appointment anymore. "I'm not bad looking," he thought, and stopped smiling at himself. He now moved his face very close to the mirror. What he saw was a dark complexioned man with brown eyes, a well-proportioned nose, fairly small lips, and black hair.

"God, I'm glad it's good in bed with her."

He picked up his watch and moved out of the bathroom and into his bedroom. It was a spacious room with a grand view of the East River. John wouldn't live in an apartment that didn't have a view. His big double bed was covered with a black and brown heavy cotton Moroccan bedspread. It had long fringes on the bottom which rested on a brown scatter rug. John moved to his double dresser and took some fresh underwear and clean socks from the top of it. "Thank God for the maid," he thought as he felt the fresh underwear close to his skin. He thought about his upcoming evening with Edith and noticed he had a small erection. With haste he slipped his hand into his jockey shorts.

He moved self-consciously to his closet, where he took out a pair of new pants and a hand-pressed sport shirt. When he was fully dressed he slipped his feet into his Gucci loafers and looked at himself in the mirror over his dresser. "I wish these pants weren't so new looking," he said with a shrug of his shoulders. He automatically picked up his watch, and as he was placing it on his wrist, he left the apartment.

As John walked through the door of his favorite steak house, he saw Edith already waiting for him. She was leaning on the end of the bar. He came up behind her and slipped his arm around her waist. Edith quickly turned her head around, a look of relief crossing her face when she saw who it was. They kissed.

"Are you ready to sit down?"

John nodded to the head waiter and they were quickly seated.

"Did you write today?"

"No. I had lunch with Sarah. She upset me so much, I didn't even attempt to work."

Before John could respond, the waiter approached for their orders.

"What's wrong with Sarah? Isn't her new roshi giving her peace?"

Edith ignored his last remark. "She's been getting these really lewd phone calls. She was sure it was Nicholas and went so far as to dress herself in a maid's uniform and stand like an idiot in the freezing cold on Fourteenth Street."

The waiter poured red wine. John nodded his head after sipping it.

"Why was she standing on Fourteenth Street in a maid's uniform?" John was incredulous, but amused by such surrealistic elements.

"Because she thought Nicholas would show up. Then they could play whore and master, I suppose. Well, no one showed up and late this afternoon she called me to say her mysterious phone friend had called again. This time she wasn't sure who it was."

"You mean she suspects someone else?"

"No, she just seemed a little less certain."

"Why would Nicholas be pretending to be someone else?"

"That's what I asked her. She said it was his way of making contact. I don't know. They had had another fight or something. I don't know."

"She sounds crazy."

Edith sighed. "Sometimes I think she is. Let's talk about something else."

"Aren't you worried about her?"

Edith was silent for a moment. "Yes, but I think I've always been worried about her. First it was her crazy marriage to Paul, a man ten years younger. Then it was her fling at Zen, then group encounter, then bread baking, then Nicholas, and now roshi, her new spiritual mentor."

"What advice did you give her?"

Their food was placed before them and Edith went after a French fry before answering. "I told her to hang up on the guy."

"What did she say to that?"

"She said she couldn't. *Please* let's talk about something else."

John began talking about his conglomerate and all the trouble certain divisions were having. At forty-four, he was one of the most successful businessmen in the country. As he spoke, Edith ate, looked at him, smiled, nodded her head, but didn't really listen. She found his business conversations cold, pragmatic and dull.

"You're not hearing a word I'm saying, are you Edith?" Edith's face reddened in embarrassment. "Sometimes I really think you're bored with me."

"No, no." She shook her head along with her denials. "Tonight in bed I'll show you how much I love you."

"You make me feel so good, Edith."

John was lying in Edith's arms. They were in her double bed and had just finished making love. Edith stroked his hair as he spoke and drifted into her own thoughts. She realized she loved being the sex object, the gorgeous whore that men both abused and worshipped. They always returned to her wanting her liberating sexuality and this was when she felt the greatest contempt. She even gave serious consideration to making them pay for it. *One thousand dollars a night.* The idea excited her. She could use the money and, even more than that, the power of it all. She'd have a triple victory: power, money, and her own indifference. The problem with John was that she cared about him. She had even come to depend on him. She had met him after his twenty-year marriage had just ended. He'd felt guilty and impotent. Edith instinctively knew his longings and gave herself to him through her fantasy life. Her lust carried them both until one day he found his own. John removed himself from Edith's arms, jolting her from her reverie.

"I think I'm going to sleep home tonight."

Edith sat up, covering her naked body with the sheet. Her face registered hurt and surprise.

"Why? You know I hate for you to leave me after we've made love."

John sat down on the edge of the bed and bent over to put on his socks. "I have a big meeting in the morning and I want to change my clothes. Just tonight, sweetheart. I'm sorry but that's the price you pay for sleeping with an American Success."

He was trying to be flip about the matter because he wasn't in the mood for dramatics. Edith decided to be understanding.

"Okay. I guess I'll have to search around for a new lover. Preferably an artist."

"That territory seems to belong to Sarah."

As John stood up to put on his clothes, Edith lit a cigarette.

"Yes, Sarah sure does love the artists. She lived with two famous painters, a writer, married a cameraman, and found Nicholas the sculptor."

"Well, since Sarah seems to have that monopoly, how about you trying a construction worker?"

John was completely dressed now and waiting for Edith to walk him to the door. She moved from the bed and kept the sheet wrapped around her body.

"You're joking, but I happen to like construction workers."

"I know you do." He kissed her gently on the cheek and squeezed her hand.

"I'll call you tomorrow. When my meeting is

over, I'll give you a call."

Edith nodded her head, opened the front door, and watched John leave. Once left alone she took a sleeping pill and flicked on her small portable television. "Maybe one of those awful made-for-TV movies is on channel two," she thought. "It might bore me enough to put me to sleep."

***

John's hand reached for the phone. It was two in the morning. The telephone number was already decided. He dialed the number. One ring, two rings, three rings. "Good, I'll get her out of a sleep, probably a sexy dream," he thought to himself.

"I'm so horny, satisfy me, I need it," he said when she answered.

"Who is this?"

Her voice was slightly indignant but not quite convincing. He knew he could push through it.

"You know who this is. Do it, honey, talk to me, tell me you love my cock."

"I do, I do."

He had her. She was fully awake now, probably touching herself. He smiled to himself and hung up the phone. Women were such easy marks, so easily teased and wanting. He looked at his cock—felt nothing. Sleep came to him; his eyes closed as a smile crossed his lips.

Sarah put down the phone and wondered why she felt disappointed that her mysterious caller had hung up. Her husband was lying next to her. She looked at him and tried to recall if he had ever excited her. Once in the first year of their marriage they had read a pornographic book together and raced to the bed for some passionate sex. That was the only time she could remember feeling excited and it hadn't even been he who'd excited her. The book had aroused her, not him, never him. The phone call aroused Sarah now and she thought about waking her husband, but decided against it. She'd rather dream in the dark about her mysterious caller, though she believed it was Nicholas. Sarah lit a cigarette and imagined her hands old and wrinkled. Maybe she was mortal after all. She had always thought of herself and her father as being immortal, but he had died a few months before and she still couldn't grasp the fact of his death. Her husband Paul had become even more abstract to her after her father's death. Sarah had married him to remain faithful to her father, but with her father gone, there was no one to be faithful to anymore. For a moment she felt a mad passion for the mysterious caller, wished for him, saw his face, dark, smiling and severe. She put out her cigarette, went deeply under the covers—as if she was joining her father underground—and went back to sleep. The next day she would dream about her caller, probably while having dinner with Paul, and feel hopeful.

The alarm rang. Sarah automatically turned it off. Paul moved slightly.

"Time to get up."

It didn't matter which one of them said those words. They were just words that were always said. Sarah wondered if just one morning nothing was said, what would happen. Maybe they both would never get out of bed again. Paul opened his eyes and looked at his wife. He spoke in half-dead tones.

"Did the phone ring in the middle of the night?"

Sarah looked at his sleepy girlish face and lied.

"No, not that I remember."

"That's funny, I could have sworn I heard you speaking with someone."

Paul got out of bed and made his way to the bathroom for his morning ritual of shower, shave, defecation, and occasional masturbation. Sarah stretched her way out of bed to make the coffee and wait her turn for the bathroom. There she would find the privacy to think about her lewd friend on the other end of the phone.

John's alarm clock also rang. He was slower than Sarah in turning it off. His sleep was a deeper one. Even when the alarm had been silenced, it took at least twenty minutes for him to make his way to the bathroom. As he shaved he thought about Edith and that he'd be seeing her tonight. John remembered the few times he and Edith had been with Sarah and Paul. He had felt a kinship with Sarah and understood her silent desires.

"Damn it," he exclaimed, noticing the small pimple of blood coming from the exact spot on his chin as it had the night before. He washed it away and thought about the wife he had divorced. He had married her, like Sarah did Paul, for safety and appearance, but not for desire or love. As Sarah loved Nicholas but couldn't move toward him, so he loved Edith, but secretly preferred emptiness. Anyhow, he didn't think Edith really loved him. She only slept with him for his money.

He glanced at his watch and quickly brushed his teeth. In some strange way the thought of Edith not loving him brought comfort. He began to hum a tune as he left the bathroom. His spirits were high. A vision of Sarah standing on the corner of Fourteenth Street brought a smile. He had watched her stand like that, maid's uniform and all, from the luxury of his heated Cadillac. He put on his brand new pin-striped suit, brushed his hair, and took a long hard look at himself in the mirror. "Not bad," he said aloud. His Mark Cross leather attache case sat waiting for him at the front door. With a whisk of his hand he picked it up and left the apartment. He whistled as he waited for the elevator. "Today is bound to be lucky," he thought. As the elevator door opened he made sure to say good morning to all the drowsy faces in the car.

John decided to walk to the office remembering, as he strolled, when he met Edith for the first time.

His greatest fear then had been impotence. He blamed it on a loveless marriage. But if he really thought about it, he would remember having had those same fears at age sixteen. Then he would only take out cheerleaders who sometimes wore dark green nail polish. Now, the first thing he did after a painful separation from his wife, was to find an excuse to go to Los Angeles. From previous business trips he knew that any man with money could always find a budding starlet to soothe his pride and reaffirm his masculinity. Without knowing it, he'd found himself involved with a hooker, adding her as a monthly expense.

Upon returning to New York and being introduced to Edith, he realized the possibility of having been used by that "sexy woman" as he described her. He remembered Edith's face when he told her that he was actually sending the woman money every month.

He justified this with an explanation.

"The few times I'd get to California, she'd pick me up at the airport. If we went somewhere, she did all the driving. I'd stay in her apartment. It was convenient, worth the money to me."

He thought about Edith's answer, which was really a question, albeit one he had never asked himself.

"Don't you think someone who liked you would do those things for nothing? Since when does friendship have to be paid for?"

He hadn't known how to answer her and regretted telling her. He'd wanted Edith's acceptance and hoped she wouldn't judge him harshly. He knew Edith wasn't particularly impressed with him that first night and in fact was involved with another man. This made it doubly crucial that he have her. He also surmised from her conversation that her writing was very important to her. Somehow he would have to find a way to make her dependent on him where she was most vulnerable.

He remembered casually mentioning on several occasions that he and a few associates were looking for tax shelters and might be interested in investing in her script. This strategy continued for six weeks, until Edith finally went to bed with him and they officially became lovers. She gave up the other man and John felt confident she was his. Edith was a lot sexier than the hooker from Los Angeles and what John now realized was that he had become dependent on her.

***

John found it challenging to be with a woman who wasn't falling all over him or demanding constant attention. His ex-wife had been that way, his sister still needed constant watching or else managed to make herself sick enough to be hospitalized, but it had been John's mother, after the death of his father, who had demanded the most from him. He could still feel her clinging to him, her arms around his neck, when he wanted to go out for the evening.

"Stay with me, John. I need you, John. You're only seventeen. There's no need to go running around at night."

John would give her a cold stare and remove her arms from his neck. She turned his heart to stone and he'd leave her lying there pleading. He felt not a drop of emotion.

It was in those late teen years that he discovered hookers and cheerleaders, and he usually sought out their company. They relieved him of the guilt he wasn't feeling and never demanded that he stay.

His mother finally remarried. It became worse for John. He slept in the room next to theirs and to this day could still hear the springs of her bed creaking and wailing as his stepfather made love to a woman who sounded as if she was gasping for life. He hated them and at twenty-one married someone with pleasant parents and made them his own. His mother died soon after, leaving a considerable fortune, which was John's father's money, to her new husband. Once more John felt betrayed—only this time he didn't run to hookers.

The real power was in business and the bigger the better. Money, appearances, love, women, power, became blurred and confused in John's mind. He really believed the American myth. If a magazine put a woman on its cover and proclaimed her a beauty, then to John she was a beauty. What he was told to desire was what he desired.

Edith did not fit into this category. She was not a model, cover girl, actress, or wife, but he desired her, almost painfully. If she hadn't had that small separation between her top front teeth, he could never have waited out the six weeks pursuing her. That blemish was one that his mother and Edith shared, and many times, when Edith smiled, he saw his mother's face and wanted to slap her. In time this feeling passed, and, without knowing it, he fell in love.

John entered his office and nodded to his secretary.

"Coffee."

His secretary was a black woman with white features. She entered with the coffee.

"Please hold all calls. I want to look over my notes for my ten o'clock meeting."

She placed the coffee down on his modern Parsinger desk and left the room. All the furniture in the large office was Parsinger, except for his Mies Van DerRohe chair. His desire for views was not restricted to his apartment alone. The view from his office window took in the entire Manhattan skyline.

As John leaned back in his chair he wondered why he had begun calling Sarah. The first time he did it, he had no intention of speaking to her. For no explainable reason, when she answered the phone, he disguised his voice, used dirty language, and suggested pornographic acts. He was shocked and aroused when she responded, though, and in retrospect, not *that* surprised. She thought he was Nicholas and John played the game, sensing her need and speaking in generalities.

"You fucking whore, I want you to suck me, lick my ass, play with my balls."

John looked down at his desk. His image looked back at him. He was on the cover of a business magazine. John smiled and opened his attache case. It was time to begin another day's work.

Sarah and Paul hadn't had much of a sex life together before their marriage. Afterward, it just about evaporated. For Sarah it was like sleeping with a younger brother and because Paul was relatively inexperienced, he left her alone hoping one day she would come to him for love.

They lived in a loft on Prince Street, even though it was more than they could afford. Sarah had wanted the space because of its light and its gracious proportions, but then no work was put into it. Paul kept his camera equipment on one side of the loft. The other side had a dining room table, four wicker chairs, and a mattress. There were lots of plants to add warmth to the large space, but no real care or time had gone into giving it a personality. It looked as if they had either just moved in or were about to move out. Paul had often mentioned doing more with the space, but Sarah resisted. She found herself almost hostile to the idea, and particularly hostile when Paul offered suggestions.

Sarah was often sick during those first years of her marriage. Paul took care of her by making sure she stayed comfortably in bed, bringing her hot tea, and cooking the meals. Sarah was grateful for the attention, if not dependent on it. The arrangement was convenient for her and she was committed to Paul for making life easy. Paul knew this about their relationship and felt sure that whatever happened she would never leave him.

Paul could arouse a deep sadness in Sarah, but she had no intention of remaining faithful to him. Opportunity struck when she met Nicholas. Paul, being a cameraman, occasionally had to be away from home. At those times, Sarah usually was not sick and often went out. It was on one of these occasions that she was introduced through Tony, a friend, to Nicholas Mejia, sculptor and *artiste extraordinaire.* He wasn't young and WASP like her husband, quite the reverse. Half-Jewish, half-Spanish, dark, and Sarah's age, Nicholas was a double-Scorpio, Sarah would later say in describing him to Edith. She felt her body come to life in his presence and wanted him for a lover.

Though Nicholas was someone unknown to Sarah, he was also deeply familiar. She immediately felt an affinity for him, as if she'd known him all of her life. He had large green eyes, which were magnified in the dimly lit restaurant where they sat. His hair was a mass of heavy black curls, almost reaching the nape of his neck. His expression was taut.

Sarah felt afraid when she first saw him. She smoked cigarette after cigarette, wanting the smoke to come between them. She didn't want to meet his gaze straight on. When she exhaled the smoke, she would allow herself to look at him. She wanted to see him through a blur. As she observed him, he smiled at her. Sarah knew he was looking at her in an approving way, and her body began to feel strange.

She felt it had meshed with his body, and at the same time, his had meshed with hers. Sarah knew his face would haunt her in her sleep. It had nothing to do with anything she could verbalize. It had nothing to do with will. Sitting next to her was a man she knew would be a perfect partner in lust. His look alone made her hands shake and her body sweat. Sexually there were no boundaries between them. It was a feeling of excitement which would be hard to contain.

Sarah could be very charming when she desired, and she used all her wiles on Nicholas that first night. After the three of them had dined together, Tony went home and Nicholas accompanied Sarah to her loft. She showed him a short art film she had made in which she appeared nude in every scene. Needless to say, Nicholas was impressed and they spent the remainder of the night in bed together. Sarah looked down at his naked body and spoke.

"Are you gentle?"

Nicholas stared straight ahead and answered, "Sometimes. Tonight I'll be gentle. It changes all the time. Every time I fuck you it will be different. We'll do whatever you want."

Sarah was aroused by his answer, but felt the need to talk.

"Good. I'm very needy. I'll probably want it all the time."

Nicholas smiled, "I'm counting on that."

Sarah rolled on top of him and stared into his face.

"I love you."

She had never said those words to her husband and here she was saying them to a perfect stranger. But to her, Paul was the stranger, he was unfamiliar. Nicholas was what she wanted to be, *"artiste extraordinaire,"* and therefore totally familiar. He also seemed to harbor enough anger for at least two and that was what Sarah found most irresistible of all.

Upon Paul's return, Sarah was twice as listless as before and only a phone call or meeting with Nicholas would energize her. He became her center and she lived for his presence. She secretly raged at Paul for depriving her of time with her lover. Paul's feeble attempts to make love to his wife were worse than a rebuttal. She froze at his touch, but did not stop him. He fondled her and she wouldn't move. Paul persisted, trying to overcome her passive resistance. With some trouble he'd penetrate her; still she wouldn't move, but, because of the darkness, he couldn't see Sarah's face. There were tears streaming from her eyes and her fists were clenched.

Sarah and Nicholas decided to go public with their affair. Their meetings became more frequent and open. Neighborhood restaurants, bars in SoHo, afternoon rendezvous in Nicholas' apartment. Paul's friends lived directly underneath and Sarah met them as she was entering Nicholas' apartment on more than one occasion. She wondered if they could hear the sound of Nicholas' bed moving to the beat of their loving. This thought satisfied her as she contemplated . . . the inevitable: How long before Paul discovered he was being made a cuckold? Paul, who cherished appearances, was to be made the fool. Sarah, who always had trouble finding work, could now dedicate herself to the full-time job of juggling two men and driving all three of them half mad.

***

Nicholas and Sarah were lying in Nicholas' bed together. It was January, about four o'clock in the afternoon. The room was in semidarkness as no one bothered to turn on the lights. Nicholas took a deep drag of his cigarette, looked directly up at the ceiling, and began to speak.

"It excites me that our love affair is illicit."

As he spoke, the inhaled smoke from his cigarette was released and Sarah followed it with her eyes as she listened. Once it had evaporated into the air, she spoke.

"Do you think we'll ever stop?"

"No. After we've risked getting caught and made love, I feel we've become one person. It's what I want."

"It's what I want, too. The excitement in you thrills me. It makes me feel so special to be loved like that."

Nicholas continued to smoke and talk at the same time.

"I've been with married women before. It meant nothing, was just an indulgence. Now, with you, it's become everything."

Sarah answered him untruthfully, "I could only be unfaithful for you."

Nicholas looked at her and smiled.

"You do it for lust. You're the lustiest woman I've ever known."

Sarah laughed.

"Tomorrow buy me something beautiful."

"Sure, baby, but right now I want to fuck you."

Nicholas reached for her and entered her body immediately. Sarah purred contentedly.

***

Paul and Sarah were expecting friends for dinner. Paul was quite sure about Sarah's affair, as word of it had reached his ears on at least four occasions. He decided to ignore it, hoping Sarah would come to her senses. It was his idea to have Robert and Linda for dinner. Sarah hadn't objected, feeling she owed Paul that little. She knew Paul would find some way to attack her if company was present. She was prepared, half looking forward to it as if she felt she deserved it.

The doorbell rang just as Paul was checking the pot roast dinner he had cooked. Paul and Sarah had decided that on this occasion he'd do the cooking and Sarah would clean up and do the dishes. Sarah went to answer the door, leaving Paul in the kitchen.

"That must be Robert and Linda. Paul, please try to keep the mess to a minimum. Remember, I have to clean it up."

Paul remained in the kitchen, barely hearing Sarah's words. He picked up a ladle to taste the sauce from his pot roast. Some of the gravy dripped on the floor. He let it stay there.

Sarah opened the door for her guests. Robert was a handsome, friendly looking man of about thirty-five. His wife, Linda, was ugly. She had a huge nose and bad skin. She was extremely neat and everything about her appearance suggested someone who took very good care of herself, except for her skin. Sarah kissed them both and they all sat down in the living room section of the loft. Paul entered from the kitchen. As he spoke he acted the role of the lighthearted host.

"What would you like, Bach, Mozart, or Vivaldi? I just bought the most beautiful horn concerto by Mozart."

Before anyone could answer, he took his new record out of its cover. "Wait until you hear this," he said with excitement.

Robert couldn't resist a little tease. "What if I want to hear something else?"

Sarah turned her head to answer Robert. She spoke with courage.

"If Paul wants to play his new record for you, what you want to hear is unimportant."

Robert felt embarrassed, knowing he had gotten himself caught in some private battle. Linda, always the compromiser, came to her husband's rescue.

"We'd love to hear your new record."

Sarah wondered why she had been hostile. Was she trying to push Paul to attack her, or was it her affair with Nicholas that was making her overtly cruel?

"How about Dewar's sours all around?" Paul asked cheerily. "I have this terrific mix."

Everyone agreed and Paul went into the kitchen to prepare the drinks. He passed them around. Sarah took a sip and stood up.

"I'm going to check the dinner."

She walked into the kitchen toward the stove. Sarah was barefoot and suddenly she felt her feet sticking to the floor. Looking down she saw the combination of mix and gravy under her feet. It was bright red, the color of blood. She just stood there, both intrigued and raging in frustration. She bent down and touched it with her hand. She lifted her hand to her face and stared at it. The sound of her husband's voice filtered into the kitchen while she stood stuck to the floor. When she finally spoke, her voice was both light and sarcastic.

"I don't know if you people can eat tonight," Sarah yelled from the kitchen. "I seem to be stuck to the floor. I guess it was too difficult for Paul to bend down and clean up his mess."

This time she had fallen for his bait and regretted her remarks. She approached her guests, not waiting for a reply to her outburst. She spoke quietly.

"Let's have dinner."

They all sat down at the dining room table. Sarah began to slice the pot roast in the kitchen. The kitchen was visible from the dining area. Paul watched his wife. Now it was his turn to speak.

"Let me slice that at the table."

"I better slice it here," Sarah responded in a persecuted voice. "The cutting board and heat will ruin the table."

Paul insisted. "I want to slice it at the table. Nothing will happen, there's a tablecloth for protection."

"I'd really prefer that you didn't."

Paul stood up and took the cutting board, with the meat on it, from under Sarah's nose and brought it back to the table. Sarah just stood there not knowing what to do. Robert and Linda watched. Sarah said nothing and returned to the table. Paul sliced the meat and served everyone from his seat.

***

Nicholas, reclining on his bed, watched Sarah put on a sheer black negligee. She had asked for a beautiful gift and he had accommodated her. In return she would perform for him. Sarah looked at herself in the long closet mirror, staring as if she was alone. Slowly she touched her breasts and her vagina, gradually transforming herself into a sex object. Her face took on a sensual quality as she turned to look at her lover.

"Like it?"

Nicholas paused a moment before speaking. "Come sit down a minute. I want to talk to you."

Sarah walked to the bed and stretched her body across from his. She was facing him.

"I don't want you to sleep with Paul anymore."

Sarah was both surprised and amused by his demand. "You know I hardly ever do."

"Hardly isn't good enough, Sarah."

Sarah laughed and pulled off her new negligee. "The thought of it seems to keep you hot."

Nicholas chuckled. "You're a real cunt."

Sarah's answer was still playful. "That's why you love me."

Nicholas lunged at her, and their playfulness turned instantly to passion.

***

"Hello, Edith, do you have a minute? I must talk to you."

Edith patiently listened at the other end of the

phone. She knew what Sarah was probably going to tell her and already felt slightly bored.

"I have a minute. What's the problem?"

"Paul bought a gun."

"What!! Did you see it, or did he tell you about it?"

"He told me, says he's going to kill Nicholas for breaking up his marriage. The only way I could calm him down was to swear I'd never see Nicholas again. Nicholas has been calling the loft and I keep hanging up on him. Oh God, he'll never forgive me."

"How can you worry about Nicholas' forgiveness when Paul sounds so out of control. You all but put that affair in skywriting. I think you'd be better off at my apartment for now. In fact, why don't you stay here tonight?"

"I don't think Paul will do anything. I'm sure it's just a threat."

"Some threat. Well, if you change your mind, please come over."

The moment Sarah put down the receiver, the phone rang again. It was Nicholas raging at her for not taking his calls, sick of her broken promises to leave her husband. He ended the conversation with a command for her to come right to his apartment. Paul wasn't home and Sarah relented. She would go there to pacify him and then quickly get back in time for Paul. Having gone through this routine so often she wasn't afraid. For one year she had successfully juggled two men.

As Sarah raced to Nicholas' apartment she fantasized spending the remainder of her life visiting Paul in jail for having killed Nicholas. In this way she'd be serving penance for her sins.

The door to Nicholas' apartment was open. Sarah walked in and found herself in total darkness. The shades were drawn and no light glowed from anywhere. She heard Nicholas breathing. The sound was coming from his bed. Sarah groped her way to her lover and lay down beside him. He said nothing. She knew not to speak but touched his body. He was naked. Instinctively Sarah knew what Nicholas wanted and silently went down with her mouth to his cock. He moaned but never touched her. It was soon over. Nicholas spoke.

"Now why don't you get out of here, you whore."

So it had come to this. Total humiliation from lover and husband.

As she entered her loft Sarah reconsidered Edith's offer to sleep there. She felt tired and used, filled with self-hate, and she couldn't face another argument with Paul. She decided to leave him a note saying where she was so he could call her and be reassured she wasn't with Nicholas.

Edith ushered Sarah into her bedroom and closed the door. They both sat down on her double bed to talk as they had done so long ago as children.

"What are you going to do with your life, Sarah?"

Sarah lit a cigarette, took a deep breath, and began to explain. "Since I've been married I feel completely dead. I'm living like a sleep-walker. I do housework, work a little on my film, and usually fall asleep reading a book at four in the afternoon. Yet I'm afraid to leave Paul. Even with Nicholas waiting for me, I'm afraid to leave him. Sometimes I think killing him would be easier than asking for a divorce. When he's sleeping, I stare at him thinking how easy it would be to smother him with my pillow. Of course, I never could, but the thought of it helps me get through the days. Nicholas gives me life and takes my pain away, and yet I don't trust him. It's strange because he's the one I think of as my husband. Yet I believe if I lived with him, he wouldn't tolerate my depressions, as Paul has. He'd probably tire of me and throw me out. Then where would I be, alone, thirty-eight, and childless?"

Edith looked at her friend. "I used to wonder why you married Paul. He always seemed a little spaced out."

Sarah answered, "Maybe that's what I like. If he's not there, I don't have to be either. It's all very safe and boring. We haven't had sex in months. I think he goes into the bathroom and masturbates. He's in there for hours."

"You really hate him."

"I guess I do, but I feel so goddamned guilty about it that it's driving me crazy."

"What kind of sex life do you have with Nicholas?"

"The time we were in California together, you remember, when Paul thought I was visiting my friend Carol?"

Edith nodded.

"We locked ourselves in the hotel room and didn't come out for nine days. That was great. We just stopped long enough to eat and sleep. Recently I'm not as turned on. Too much sneaking around, tension, guilt, the usual shit. Now he hates me so much he treats me like a whore."

Edith began to feel hungry. "Let's go to the kitchen and make some dinner."

The two women left the bedroom and happily immersed themselves in the mindless ritual of preparing a good meal.

***

John began calling Sarah more and more frequently. He was no longer as cool as before. He was like a junkie in need of a fix. He would leave a business luncheon early, giving one excuse or another, only to find himself running to his office in a cold sweat. Then he would enter his sanctuary and lock the door. John felt ashamed of what he knew he was going to do. First he'd sit at his desk and rationalize. "I'm not hurting anyone. I just must speak to Sarah. But why am I so disgusting, vulgar, coarse?"

Sweat gathering in the palms of his hands, his forehead turning hot and cold, he would light cigarettes only to put them out, and, finally, inevitably, he would make the phone call.

"Hello."

"Who is this?" Her tone was stern.

"It's Tony. I thought you might be missing me. I know you want my cock . . . almost as much as I'd love to lick your pussy."

Sarah was nervous. Could this man really be Nicholas? She suddenly felt ashamed.

"Please don't call me anymore." Sarah spoke these words kindly.

John was silent. Sarah hung up the receiver and cried.

***

John and Edith were lying naked in John's double bed.

"I'd love to prostitute you to other men."

Edith looked up at him with an expressionless face. "Tell me how it goes."

His words came quickly. "I see us living in an old stone castle in Europe. I'm lazy and you're my wife. Each day I send you to another man. You fuck him and bring the money home to me."

Edith spoke. "In other words, you're a classy pimp and I'm a hooker."

"No, that's not exactly right. You're cultured, rich, and charming."

Edith felt John's cock harden and moved herself

on top of him. As her motion carried her up and down, she whispered into his ear, "You mean we've both got class, but what I really want to know is what you do while I'm out fucking other men."

John laughed and plunged deeply into her. "Sleep."

***

John bought himself a dog. It was a spaniel, a cocker spaniel. On a few occasions he even brought the dog to work with him. His secretary took Gino out for his afternoon walk and the rest of the time he ran around the office. John loved it when important businessmen fussed over the dog, beaming like a proud parent if Gino received a compliment. Whenver he ate in a restaurant, a doggy bag was always prepared. John instructed the waiter to take back the leftover food from everyone's plate for the dog. In his free time he taught Gino tricks and no matter the hour, his pet was taken outside for his nightly walk. There were even times that John would have preferred the company of his dog to being with Edith. Gino always loved him, never spoke back, and was forever faithful. Recently, John found Edith testy, at moments downright hostile. He couldn't bear the thought of losing control over her and the more he felt her pulling away, the more he bullied her.

"What do you mean you can't meet me?"

"I'm in the middle of writing and don't want to stop."

"I'll think you don't care about me unless you see me now."

"Think what you wish."

Thank God he didn't have those problems with Gino. The dog obeyed and adored him. John felt complimented when people told him he and his dog looked alike. Edith told him that once to be mean. He ignored her, thinking her jealous. On Saturday afternoons he'd take Gino out for long walks. From the look on his face, one would have thought he was pushing a baby carriage instead of holding a dog on a leash. Occasionally John stopped and spoke to other people with dogs. He'd leave them confirmed in his opinion that Gino was the best. Since purchasing his dog, John's desire for dirty phone calls had decreased. Gino slept on the end of the bed. John was embarrassed to get up in the middle of the night to call a woman. After all, his dog was watching.

***

Edith finally received an acceptance for one of her short stories. A respectable magazine was going to publish it. Edith felt good and with this feeling came a desire to leave John. The dream that he might become a warm presence for her was strong and hard to give up. To let go of him meant being alone, and this thought both frightened her and made her feel strong. When frightened, she saw herself as two feet tall, hunched over behind a closed door. This image made her feel sad. Her strength had enabled her to persevere with her writing and have friends. Maybe it *was* time to be alone.

She called John to give him the good news.

"I'm coming right over. I have something wonderful to tell you."

"What's happened?"

"I'll tell you when I get there."

He opened the door for her and could sense her exuberance. He noticed her usually perfect hair was messy and that she was in a sweat. They sat down on the living room couch together, John looking at her quizzically.

"Well, what's all the excitement about?"

"Kenneth Lurie has accepted my latest short story. I'm really thrilled."

Edith took a cigarette from John's well-supplied cigarette box on the coffee table. Her hand shook slightly as she lit it. John watched but said nothing. Edith continued to speak.

"He's the first person willing to take a risk on my work. Everyone else has said how original and interesting it was, but he's doing more than just talking. I can't believe it. He's actually going to publish it."

John stood up and began to pace the room.

"That's terrific news. I always knew you would get what you wanted."

"You did, John? I never thought you had that much confidence in me."

John stopped pacing and looked at Edith, who was flicking the ashes from her cigarette.

"You're an achiever. I'm proud of you. Now why don't we go into my bedroom and make love?"

Edith looked surprised. "After what I've just told you, I'd think you'd understand my head is somewhere else and I'm too excited. My thoughts aren't on sex. You should be able to understand that."

"You're so fidgety, Edith. It's making me nervous. Why don't you lie down with me for a few minutes?"

"I'm not fidgety. I'm happy and I don't want to lie down. Can't we celebrate by having a nice lunch and talking instead of fucking?"

"I'm really happy for you, but if all I wanted was a nice lunch, I'd be with someone else."

Edith looked at John in a rage.

"I'll speak to you next week."

She walked out of the apartment, banging the door behind her. Her joy turned to pain when she realized how indifferent John was to her feelings and good fortune. It reminded her of times at college when she'd call her mother with happy news. Invariably she was misunderstood and hung up the phone in disappointment and tears. This time, though, Edith was determined to fight and enjoy her moment of acceptance. As she rushed through the streets she noticed a tall blond man with a beard standing on a busy corner. He was shouting about something and carrying a sign. Edith was curious and walked closer to hear his voice.

"Save the whales. Save the whales."

It was almost a chant. Edith looked at the man and he smiled at her. She felt touched.

"Save the whales. Save the whales. One is killed every nineteen minutes."

Edith quickly signed her name to a petition and continued walking. As she entered her apartment she could still hear the chant.

"Save the whales. Save the whales."

Suddenly Edith felt like crying.

***

John actually knew how Edith felt, having returned home many a night to his wife's demands for love and unable to give because he was preoccupied with his work or on his own high from it. Either way she was excluded. Now, when he'd been excluded, he took it personally and didn't like it. He felt that the more successful Edith became, the less need she'd have for him. "I'll call her and apologize," he thought. "Maybe buy her a gift." John liked the second idea and quickly left his apartment.

On his way to Tiffany's, he bumped into a tall blond man screaming something about whales. "What an idiot, shouting like that in the street," he thought. He quickened his pace, anxious to get out of earshot.

***

Sarah was genuinely happy for her friend. It also forced her to recognize how little work she had accomplished in the last two years. Paul, Nicholas, phone calls, an editing job here and there, what did it all mean? Her own personal work she had let slide. If she died that moment the only thing she'd have to show for her thirty-eight years was a ten-minute art film. Edith didn't seem to feel pain the way she did. It was always with Sarah, dictating her life. Every time she thought of leaving Paul, the pain went through her. Her false promises to Nicholas caused him agony but her only reaction was to be afraid of his bad temper. She felt she had not been unfaithful to Paul because she had remained married to him. Her affair had provided Sarah with enough guilt to stay with Paul for a lifetime, punishing him along the way for preventing her from being with the man she really loved. Edith seemed to be taking on life, which made Sarah hopeful. After all, aren't our friends a reflection of ourselves?

She suddenly remembered how jealous she had always been of Edith. In high school Edith was the popular one, the prettier one, the one people adored. After college Sarah purposely hadn't seen Edith for a few years. She had wanted to find her own identity and in this way feel strong enough to have a friendship with equality. She called Edith only after she was living with a world-famous painter, inviting Edith to visit her and her celebrated lover in East Hampton. It hadn't worked out as Sarah had hoped. Her artist got drunk, made a pass at Edith, and threw potato salad in Sarah's face.

Sarah felt a sudden urge to masturbate. She lay down on her bed and tried touching herself. She quickly took her hands off her body, feeling ashamed. She then tried rubbing her thighs together. Nothing. Not being able to conjure up any fantasies didn't help matters, but Sarah had no fantasy life. Men, and particularly Nicholas, had always provided that for her. Even in total privacy she couldn't let her mind go free. The dirty phone calls stimulated her, everyone's rage stimulated her, but in all her thirty-eight years nothing had stimulated her to orgasm. She often thought that had she been able to have an orgasm with Nicholas, she might have left Paul. Sarah was holding on to something for dear life, never realizing that the end result could only be death.

***

Paul and Sarah sat facing each other eating their Chinese dinner from containers.

"How come you can't have dinner ready when I get home? You know how hungry I get."

Sarah looked at him, hiding her anger. Her tone was condescending when she answered. "Sorry, I got delayed. How was work today?" Paul was the cameraman on an industrial film at the moment.

"Goddamn Lawrence. He must have made me do the same shot six times. Thought I'd go crazy."

Sarah felt very bored with Paul's work story, but feigned interest.

"Did you finally get what he wanted?"

"I did all right. I almost got run over trying to get the right angle, and he made a big joke out of it."

Sarah answered, "He was probably just trying to be funny. I wouldn't take it seriously. You know, it is rather amusing."

Sarah's remark made Paul angry and his tone was hostile as he spoke.

"I don't find my practically being killed amusing." His voice grew angrier. "I bet you'd really like it if something happened to me. Maybe you'd even stop being frigid. Who knows, stranger things have happened. You might become a swinger. Yeah, I can see you, a real swinger."

Sarah stopped eating. She knew she was being attacked because of her affair with Nicholas, but still felt hurt and surprised.

"What brought this on? You're getting your people mixed up. It wasn't me who made the joke, it was your director. Why don't you go scream at him?"

With that Sarah got up from the table and left the loft. Paul didn't try to stop her. He remained at the table staring into space. Sarah went directly to a public phone booth and called Nicholas. She didn't give him a chance to speak, just announced that she was coming over.

Nicholas opened the door for her. Sarah immediately spoke in a slightly shaky voice.

"You didn't seem very surprised to hear from me."

"Why should I be? I knew you'd call. How about a drink, Sarah? You look like you could use one."

Nicholas handed her a vodka and they sat down on separate chairs.

"I knew you wouldn't mind my coming here when you called last night and hung up."

"I never called you last night. I've vowed not to call or see you till you move out on Paul. I didn't even want you here tonight."

Sarah's voice was secure as she spoke. "It's hard for me to believe that after all the sexy phone conversations we've been having the past few months."

"Sarah, I don't know what you're talking about, but I don't make dirty phone calls. It's not my style. Sounds more like something Paul would do."

Sarah was in a state of shock, unable to comprehend that her caller wasn't Nicholas, yet somehow knowing she had suspected another person all along. To hear him say it made her suspicions a reality and this filled her with self-disgust. She rationalized, telling herself that he was lying. Yet, if there was one thing Nicholas wasn't, it was a liar. Her humiliation and shame were so great that she felt revulsion at being in Nicholas' apartment. She stood up to leave and walked to the door. Tears welled in her eyes as she turned to go.

"I thought it was you. I thought it was you."

She banged the door closed and ran home, knowing Paul would greet her with loving arms. That night there were no phone calls, which made Sarah once more believe that possibly it really was Nicholas. This thought comforted her while she spent most of the night in the bathroom vomiting.

***

"Sarah, I've missed you."

It was two o'clock in the morning. The phone had just rung and Sarah quickly picked it up, not wanting Paul to be awakened. Sarah's voice was angry.

"Just who are you?"

"You know who I am. I'm your lover."

"You better cut the shit and tell me who this really is or I'm going to hang up and report these calls to the police."

"Sarah, let's talk about your cunt."

Sarah banged the phone down, shaking with

humiliation. As she lay down on her bed, she felt scared. What if it really was Nicholas? And if it wasn't, would she miss this pervert too? She fell asleep wishing she were dead.

John was surprised at Sarah's reaction to him on the phone and realized she must have found out that her caller was not Nicholas. John suspected, however, that Sarah would prefer the lie, so perhaps all was not lost. He'd continue calling until once more she thought he was her lover.

***

"Paul needs to find a trailer for a film he's shooting for German television."

Edith thought a moment before responding to Sarah.

"I bet John could help you. His company out west makes mobile homes and trailers. Why don't you call him? He'll remember who you are and probably love to help."

"That's a good idea. What's the name of his company?"

"The Johns' Group. His partner's name is also John."

"That's a disgusting name."

"I guess it is, but I'm sure he'll be helpful."

Sarah hung up the phone and found John's number in the directory. She called. The secretary asked for her number. He'd call back.

John was in his office when his secretary buzzed to say that a friend of Edith's was on the phone, Mrs. Sarah Naughton. John froze and said he was busy.

"Take her number and I'll call back."

He sat at his desk, terrified. Had she found out? Did she want a confrontation, possibly blackmail? He'd have to return the call but then she might recognize his voice. He decided to have his secretary call back and ask the nature of her call. John left instructions and went to lunch. It was hard for him to eat. As he sat alone in the restaurant he practiced different sounds with his voice just in case he needed to disguise it. Upon his return to the office his secretary informed him of Sarah's wishes.

"She wanted to know if her husband could rent a trailer cheap for a film he's doing."

John was so relieved he instructed his secretary to have Sarah and her husband come to his office to work something out. He'd be only too happy to help. His curiosity had also gotten the better of him. He wanted to see the woman he'd been abusing on the telephone. In a certain way he loved her. If only he could remember what she looked like. John wasn't afraid of Sarah recognizing his voice in person. After all, one did sound different on the phone. He anticipated their visit with excitement.

***

John welcomed Sarah and Paul into his grand office. Sarah spoke first.

"This view is fantastic. Here, Paul and I thought you could use a little plant, but I see you have more than enough."

John took the gift.

"Thank you. I never have enough plants."

He was genuinely moved by Sarah's gesture. John's guests sat down. Paul took the cigar John offered, giggling silently with the thrill of feeling rich. Sarah observed her husband with some surprise. She hadn't realized how much Paul loved money. She knew his panic when he wasn't making it, but felt that was natural. Only recently did she notice his bourgeois side. He had bought himself a Pierre Cardin suit and was talking of moving into a cooperative apartment farther uptown.

Paul was the son of a Midwestern minister and a social worker mother. His idea of success was to make a lot of money in the big city. The only thing that made him different from John was their professions. One was a businessman, the other a filmmaker. But as Sarah observed them laughing and puffing on their big cigars together, she realized they were interchangeable. Nicholas could never be seduced, but Paul was just waiting. The artist wanted to be the businessman and the businessman wanted to be the artist. She could almost hear John describing their visit to an associate. He'd be grinning like a Cheshire cat.

"Just had a filmmaker in my office. Wanted to know about renting a trailer cheap. I told him he could have one for nothing. Wouldn't charge an artist."

Sarah wondered if her evaluation of John was correct and would ask Edith to confirm it. Something else about him was both odd and familiar. His voice. She knew it and wondered why. Sarah hadn't seen John for a long time. Why should she know his voice? As Sarah continued to have these thoughts, John and Paul completed their deal for the trailer. John would call his top man in Colorado and make sure Paul got one for nothing. As John walked his guests to the office door, he turned to Sarah.

"Have you seen Edith recently?"

"Last week. You must be taking good care of her, John. She looked great."

"Do you think she's in love?"

Sarah laughed. "That's not for me to say."

John's face reddened as he spoke. "I always thought I'd be the man in her life."

Sarah answered him honestly. "I think that up until now you have been."

John said nothing and smiled. "I'll call my man in Colorado and get back to you with the arrangements."

They all shook hands and separated. Sarah was puzzled and Paul was pleased.

***

Edith was visiting Sarah in her editing room, eating sandwiches that she'd brought for lunch.

"I get the feeling that John is very involved with you. He got emotional when he asked about you. His voice changed."

Edith answered, but Sarah wasn't listening. "I'm sure he cares more for me than any other woman, but that's not saying much."

Edith observed her friend. "What are you thinking about?"

"His voice. It was so familiar."

"Speaking of voices, do you still get those dirty phone calls?"

Sarah jumped. That was it.

"That's the voice. If I didn't know better, I'd say John's been the one calling me."

Edith was incredulous. "That's impossible. Why would he do such a thing? John may be cold and unfeeling, but he's not a degenerate."

"If he ever calls again, I'll tape him. I want you to hear the voice."

"Was there anything else he said or did to give you that impression?"

"No. He just appeared self-conscious and uncomfortable."

"I'm sure he was. He must have wanted to please you terribly."

"Yes, but only because we were your friends."

"And because Paul is a filmmaker," Edith added.

"I'm curious to see if those calls start again."

"Sarah, you're crazy. I hope you do get a call. I'd like to know what you're talking about."

Edith left her friend to return home. She decided to walk crosstown instead of taking the bus. It was hard for her to fathom the implications of Sarah's impression. John, wealthy, respectable, frightened, making pornograhic phone calls to her best friend. Even doing it when they were lovers. Edith felt a lump in her throat that hurt her whole head. She needed to get home and take a couple of aspirin. It began to rain heavily but Edith continued to walk, oblivious to the fact that she was getting soaked. The man chanting "Save the whales" stood at his usual corner holding up his sign. He, too, seemed oblivious to the rain. Edith walked quickly by him. If only the pain would leave her head, she could think more clearly. Edith finally reached home, took off her wet clothes, took two aspirin, and got into a hot bath. She wanted to cleanse herself, but wondered if it would ever be possible to get all the dirt off.

***

John felt proud of the way he'd handled Sarah and Paul. He was certain he'd made a good impression. Getting them a free trailer was more than they'd hoped for; he'd have to be labeled a "good guy." He also couldn't help feeling slightly smug at having Sarah in his office. He knew her secrets but she didn't know it. Sarah looked better than he remembered, but he felt no physical attraction toward her. Even when she waited for him in the maid's uniform, he hadn't wanted her. It was the idea he loved. He thought once more about initiating a phone call. He decided to wait a while. Best not to push one's luck. John buzzed his secretary.

"Is the dog out there with you? Well, would you please bring him here."

The door to his office quickly opened. Gino jumped onto John's lap and lay there quietly. John lit a cigar and thought about business.

***

John could wait no longer. His need to call Sarah was too great. Little did he know that Sarah had a tape device set up to her phone and was just waiting to hear his voice.

The phone rang. It was late at night. Paul was asleep.

"Hello."

"Hi."

With her free hand Sarah clicked on the tape recorder.

"Who is this?" Her tone was stern.

"We haven't spoken in a long time. I thought you might be missing me. I know you want my cock . . . almost as much as I'd love to lick your pussy."

Sarah was horrified. Could this man really be John? If it were, she didn't know which one of them should feel more ashamed. Her voice become kind.

"Look, I think I know who you are. Please don't call anymore."

John was silent.

Sarah hung up the phone and cried. There must be some mistake, she thought. There must be some mistake. All those months of believing it was Nicholas when in reality it was probably her best friend's lover. She wiped the tears from her eyes. Edith would know for certain. She'd play the tape for her tomorrow and then destroy it. She felt a surge of pity for John. Or was it for herself?

The two women met in Sarah's loft.

"You want a drink?"

Edith responded with a nod of her head.

"Wine?"

"Yes. I'd prefer red if you have it."

"He called and I want you to hear it. Tell me if it sounds like John to you."

"Is that why you got me here?"

"Yes. I was afraid you might not come if I told you in advance."

"The whole thing is a little sickening."

Edith sipped her wine and stared straight ahead. She didn't want to look at Sarah. She hated her for putting her through this ordeal and yet was curious. She even felt jealous. It was something John and Sarah had done behind her back which hadn't included her. They had been verbally intimate. And even though Sarah thought she was talking to her lover, John knew precisely who he was calling. What's more, he'd been calling her throughout their entire affair. These thoughts brought severe trembling to Edith's body. She was furious.

Sarah looked at Edith. "Ready?"

"No, not yet."

Edith continued to sip her wine. She wondered if Sarah wasn't a little too anxious for her to hear the tape. Maybe all those envious years in high school were still with her. There was no point in putting it off any longer.

"Okay, let's hear it."

Sarah pressed a button.

"Hello."

"Hi."

"Who is this?"

"We haven't spoken in a long time. I thought you might be missing me. I know you want my cock . . . almost as much as I'd love to lick your pussy."

"Look, I think I know who you are. Please don't call anymore."

Sarah clicked off the tape and looked at Edith. She looked as if a vampire had sucked out all her blood. She was white. Sarah had never seen her this way. Edith tried to speak but her rage choked her. She said nothing for minutes.

"Was that John's voice?"

"Yes."

"God, he's pathetic."

Edith looked at her. "And so are you."

She stood up and walked out of the loft.

Sarah crouched over in pain. She wondered if her friend would ever speak to her again. Why hadn't she left it alone? Gradually, she was losing everyone she loved. Edith would forgive her but something would be irretrievably lost between them. Sarah wanted to die. She threw the tape in the garbage and stared at the clock. Edith would be arriving home soon. She'd watch the time and call her in half an hour. That thought comforted her as the minutes ticked by.

Edith arrived home furious and frightened. She felt as if she were surfacing from underground. Her life had gone on beneath the dirt and only now, gasping for air, did she know it. She took off her clothes and put on a bathrobe. It was dreamlike. Her body felt separated from her. She was outside of herself, observing, estranged. The phone rang.

"Hello."

It was Sarah calling to repent. Edith didn't want to deal with her friend's remorse.

"I don't want to talk about it now. A friend's coming over and I have to get ready. We'll talk tomorrow."

Edith sat down at her desk and wrote two notes. One to John and one to Sarah. Both said the same thing.

> *I'm going to Europe for a while. For the moment I can offer no explanation other than the fact that I need to leave New York. I'll call you when I return.*
>
> *Edith*

She put each letter in an envelope and sealed them closed. She then picked up the phone and made a reservation for the first flight leaving the next morning for Paris.

Edith left on the sixth of July. She hadn't been to Paris in three years. Her last trip had been purely for pleasure. She'd met a lot of people and had a good time. Her address book from that trip rested securely in her handbag; even if it weighed her down a bit, it was safer than in a suitcase.

"Thank God Philippe will be there to meet me," she thought as she boarded the plane. Edith had met him through mutual friends and had called him after she'd booked her flight. He had offered to pick her up. He also said he would try to find her an apartment. Considering that Edith had only seen him on four occasions three years before, she was very touched by his consideration. He was a doctor and they had kept in touch by mail, but not with any regularity.

The trip was basically to get away from John and Sarah, but she planned to show one of her scripts around while abroad. "It's always good to take some work along," she reflected. "It's like traveling with a friend."

In truth she was frightened. Her discovery of

John's secret perversion scared her into wondering if she really knew or could trust anyone. It took on nightmare proportions. Edith found herself thinking he might be capable of anything, even murder. The time away would almost be a test to see if she could get over her fear. As she sat on the plane, she wondered if she would be afraid of being alone on the Paris streets. There wouldn't be good friends to call and no safe apartment to return to each day. When she had made her flight reservation the night before, there had been something a little unreal about it; she didn't quite connect herself with a ticket to Paris. But here she was on her way. Edith tried not to think of the people she had left behind. This was to be her experience and she wanted her mind as free from worry as possible.

Philippe was waiting at the gate. He looked older and more sure of himself than she remembered, but his face bore a certain mask of propriety which seemed to hide cruelty or, perhaps, fear. She couldn't tell if he were shy or cold. Yet he had been very considerate and found her an apartment for two weeks. After that, she was on her own.

They drove quietly to Paris in Philippe's car. After a while he broke the silence. "You know, I was asked to lecture in Moscow on tropical diseases."

Edith responded with enthusiasm. "That's some compliment. All your work really paid off."

Even as Edith spoke, she began to feel inadequate next to Philippe and his success. For an instant she wanted to impress Philippe—tell him what she did, who she knew—but as the words tumbled out of her, as if beyond control, she started hating herself. Best to make small talk.

"I don't remember all these high rises here before. It's a shame the world is becoming so Americanized."

Philippe answered in a serious voice, "Paris is still sacred."

Edith looked out the car window and hoped it was true.

They reached the apartment, sat down, and spoke in relaxed tones. Their conversation was friendly and intimate. Nothing important was said, but it didn't matter. Philippe finally got up to go, leaving Edith to discover her new surroundings. She was strangely calm. She puttered about the apartment, unpacked, made some tea, and felt peculiarly abstract. It was as if it were not she who was present, but rather another person she might be watching in a movie.

After a while, the phone rang. The unexpected sound made her jump. It was Philippe being considerate and making sure she was all right in the apartment. Edith assured him that all was well and there went her mouth again, saying things she did not mean.

"I'm fine, please don't feel you have to take care of me and don't let my presence in Paris impose on your time."

She said the opposite of everything she felt, when really she had to say nothing at all.

He was silent, which made her speak even more—"How good it was to see you; thank you for your kindness . . ."

Again he said nothing. Then, after a pause, "Are you fine?"

"I'm great. We'll speak tomorrow."

It was awkward. When she hung up, she wondered why such babbling was necessary. Insecurity overwhelmed her. She wished he hadn't called and been so damned considerate. Those things were hard to handle. It was difficult for Edith to be natural with him because he was basically a stranger. She had come to Paris and wanted to be totally herself, and after being there for only an hour she was already being someone else. This had to stop immediately. Edith wanted to be with Philippe but didn't want to impose and that was what she had tried to say. "I do hope it came out all right." She went to the kitchen and found a can of nuts. She ate one and it was bad. It sat wrong in her stomach.

The next day Edith could do nothing but sleep. Every time she tried to do something, she fell back on the couch to sleep. Was it fear, utter exhaustion, or just a good depression? She felt lonely. She had no real connection with anyone in Paris, and everyone in the States was far away. She wondered if she had ever been connected to anyone—anywhere.

Edith forced herself to bathe, get dressed, go out. The streets were empty, the stores boarded closed for lunch, and she couldn't wait to return to the apartment. Once again, safely inside, she called Philippe, hoping he would invite her for dinner. He did and Edith was relieved. But still she had to sleep. It was as if years of tension wouldn't permit her to keep her eyes open.

The door bell rang, jolting her awake. It was Philippe. He stood there holding a bag of food.

"The restaurant I wanted to take you to was closed, so I thought it would be nice for us to eat home."

For some reason Edith didn't believe him, and felt angry, but showed nothing.

"I'll warm up the food and you set the table," she said.

Philippe did as he was told and in a little while they were eating dinner on the terrace of the apartment.

"Do you think you'll ever marry?"

Without hesitation Philippe shook his head.

"Why?"

"Just too many possibilities for new experiences to tie yourself down to one person."

"Sometimes I feel that way but other times the thought of growing old alone frightens me."

"I don't think about it."

Edith watched Philippe as he ate and knew they would make love that night. He knew it too and there was a sweet, unspoken sensuality between them for the rest of the dinner. They cleared the dishes and quite naturally made their way to the bedroom.

"I'm a bloody mess tonight. I hope you don't mind."

"I don't mind."

They made love three times and then Edith felt he wanted to leave her. Somewhere she had suspected he might, so her disappointment was not too great.

"You sure you don't want to sleep here? It's awfully late to go home."

"It's best that I go. I need my bag for the hospital first thing in the morning. I'd rather leave now."

When he left, Edith thought she would never see him again. They had given each other what was needed for the moment and it was enough. There was nothing more for the two of them; the sex was good but the connection gone.

It was sad because they could have been good friends and lovers. No, of course that was not true. It was her wish, but like all wishes, it was based more on hope than reality. Edith felt afraid. It always felt lonely to give up a fantasy. Once more she must face herself and go on to other experiences. The next day she was to meet Michel, someone she was supposed to have called on her previous trip but had never gotten around to. This time she made a point of speaking to him.

***

Edith's first impression of Michel that evening was that he was a man capable of suicide. When he opened the door for her, she was too out of breath from climbing the five flights of steps to his apartment really to notice him. She saw the couch in his living room, moved quickly by him, and sat down immediately. It took her about five minutes of pure stillness to take in her surroundings and the man who lived so high up the stairs.

"I hope you don't think I'm rude for running directly to your couch, but I can't breathe. In America, we have elevators," she sarcastically added.

Michel didn't answer, but it was obvious to Edith that he was studying her, almost dissecting her.

"Would you like some wine?"

"Great."

Michel moved to the kitchen while Edith stayed glued to the couch. Her mind was already moving in a hostile direction. I'm not going to offer to help him after climbing up those goddamn steps. He put the wine down along with some sliced cheese placed neatly on a cheese board. It was a white wine which he poured into two elegant wine glasses.

"Here, drink this. You'll feel better."

Edith didn't know why, but she felt he had said these words and gone through the same motions many times. Ritual, that's what it felt like. She took the glass from him and for the first time looked into his face. It was aristocratic in a German way but it told very little. His eyes were blue and she noticed that one of them was glass. How strange. His nose was long, his lips thin. Straight blond hair, parted in the middle, straggled down the sides of his face.

"What wonderful wine," she said as her eyes

traveled about the apartment. Nothing was out of order. Everything had its place, as if the objects in the apartment were born there and never had been moved. There were big oil paintings of naked grotesque women which interfered with the sterility of their setting.

"Do you paint?"

"I'm an art director but someday hope to give it up to be an artist."

"Are these your paintings?"

"No, a friend of mine from New York did them. Do you like them?"

"They're exotic and quite beautiful."

As they spoke, Michel looked directly at her and kept filling their glasses. He poured the wine as if the only thing he had ever done in his life was pour wine.

"How long ago did you leave Germany?"

"I've been living in Paris for twelve years."

"Do you ever go back?"

"Yes. At least once a year I visit with my parents."

Edith was beginning to feel drunk. She did not find this tall, glass-eyed German very sensual, and though he had said nothing strange, she was intrigued by his strangeness.

"I spent the entire morning in some damn French post office trying to get a telegram off to my friend. Today is her birthday."

"Today is my birthday too."

"How funny. How old are you?"

"Thirty-eight today."

"We're both the same age. Both born in 1942,

and you and my friend Sarah on the same day. That intrigues me, it really does."

"Maybe it's a miracle."

By now they were both hungry.

"Where would you like to eat?"

"This is your city. Wherever we go is fine with me."

Somehow Edith's tone and language sounded coarse. She thought herself common next to this soft spoken German gentleman. She never remembered feeling that way with John. Though they had decided to leave for dinner, neither of them moved.

"Have you ever met an angel?"

For some reason Michel's question didn't surprise her. Edith answered, "I think if one were sitting on my lap I wouldn't see it."

"It's hard to see angels, isn't it?"

"Real angels are difficult to find. You have to be ready to see them."

"Yes, but I think they're all around us."

"They probably are. It's a nice thought."

Edith finally stood up and brought the glasses into the kitchen. She noticed the beautiful Italian pottery plates and bowls. The silverware looked like a family heirloom. It was all so perfect and tasteful. She thought about her own glasses back home. Most of them were empty jam bottles or glasses she had managed to swipe from hotel bathrooms. Again she felt rather common, but decided to put these feelings aside and enjoy a good French diner with an exiled German. Both of them had been born the same year, she a Jew, he a

German. A wave of hate passed through her.

"We'd better go. It's getting late. The only decent place open now is Copain's," he said. "I know it's a bit noisy but it does have a certain atmosphere."

Edith realized she was supposed to know what Copain's was.

"Oh, Copain's is fine with me."

She was doing it again, pretending.

The restaurant was lit as if for a movie. In fact, it was the place where people came to be seen. Michel and Edith were seated. The bright lights made her feel vulnerable. She was sure Michel was looking at the pores of her skin and that her makeup was too obvious and that perhaps she even looked like a hooker.

"You know, you look very Mediterranean."

"Do I? A lot of people tell me I look French."

"No, your eyes are Mediterranean."

Edith began to sneeze.

"You'll forgive me if I put my dark glasses on? They prevent my eyes from tearing."

Suddenly Michel left the table. Edith continued to sneeze behind the dark glasses. She knew Michel would be back and his absence didn't bother her. He quickly returned with a small packet of Kleenex bought at a drugstore. Edith couldn't decide if he was being considerate or was just afraid she might embarrass him if forced to use the restaurant napkin on her nose. Why did she feel so ordinary next to this man? Her sneezing stopped as quickly as it had started, but the dark glasses remained.

"A toast to your birthday. I think we should drink to angels."

Michel lifted his glass and clicked it against Edith's.

"To angels. Do you think you could see one with your dark glasses on?"

Michel ordered for both of them. His French was beautiful, perfect, like everything else he had acquired.

"How has it been for you alone in Paris?" he asked Edith.

"Sometimes good, other moments frightening. That's one of the reasons I came alone. I wanted to see if I could get past my fear."

"You know, I have a beautiful house near the sea in Morocco. I never used it much because I was afraid to go to the ocean by myself. I thought I'd feel very lonely. One day I decided it was really stupid of me, so I mustered all my strength and went to Morocco alone. I set a schedule for each day at the water. The first day I tried staying there for ten minutes. It felt like ten hours and I looked at my watch the entire time. The second day I stayed for twenty minutes and even ventured a little into the ocean. The third day I stayed an hour and began to notice the other people on the beach. By the fourth day I made friends with a little boy and we went swimming together. The days after that were easy. I would leave my watch at home and spend all my time at the ocean."

"What did you learn from that experience?"

"That I can now go to the ocean by myself."

Michel's story made Edith laugh. She had

expected such a profound answer. All he did was plunge into the fear.

"How is your dinner?"

"I haven't had a bad meal in Paris yet."

"One evening," Michel spoke with pride, "you'll have to let me cook for you. I'm a gourmet chef."

"The French really do carry on about food, don't they?"

"For me, food is a religion. Don't you think it's very important?"

Edith didn't know quite how to answer. She never gave much thought to food one way or the other. She ate what she liked, cooked simply, and wouldn't dream of preparing anything too taxing. When she was a little girl, food had been very important to her mother: the preparation of meals, the slaving over fresh vegetables, the fresh chickens. She could see her mother's expression as she mechanically cleaned and plucked out the feathers of a chicken. The look on her face was removed and depressed when preparing those hateful meals. Every now and then she'd remember what her hands were doing and attack the bird, pulling it apart as if it were some human she wanted to kill. At dinner Edith would have to eat that despised chicken and say how much she enjoyed it. It was much easier to pretend. Edith came out of her reverie.

"Yes, food is important. It's not my religion, but it is important."

"Would you like to go somewhere to dance, or are you too tired?"

"No, I'd like to go dancing."

"I'm not allowed in many of the more well-known discotheques in Paris."

Edith didn't ask him why. She didn't want to know. He told her anyway.

"I used to get drunk a lot and act up. I hated those places and the women I was with. That's all over now."

Edith wondered of just how many fears and eccentricities this strange, willful German had managed to cure himself.

They went to a small discotheque off St. Germain. It was dark and almost empty. Edith removed her dark glasses. A man sat in a corner watching his date dancing by herself on the dance floor. Every now and then his head bobbed up and down as he tried to keep himself awake. The music was all American but Edith knew very few of the songs or performers. Occasionally a familiar record was played and a longing for New York came over her. The two of them never did get up to dance. Edith was happy for that. To have danced with Michel would have been more awkward than romantic. He was aristocratic but not graceful. She suspected his lack of grace might possibly rub off on her, making her feel clumsy. Better they sit, talk, and continue drinking.

"It's four o'clock in the morning. I better get you home."

As they left, Edith noticed the woman still dancing alone. Her escort could no longer watch her. He had fallen asleep.

They got into a taxi and Michel gave the driver

her address. He took her hand in a friendly way. It had been a nice night and Edith felt more attracted to him than she had thought possible. When they reached her apartment, she was surprised when Michel got out of the taxi with her. They went upstairs, sat on the couch, and watched the sun come up. It was then she knew she would become Michel's angel, or at least that's what he would believe. She suspected that John had thought of her as an angel too.

But Edith was tired of being an angel; it was too complicated. It meant a denial of herself, her anger, all to be the beloved angel. "Mirror, mirror on the wall, Who's the fairest of them all?" The image of her mother plucking at that ugly chicken and staring out the window came to her. "Mirror, mirror on the wall, Who's the fairest of them all?"

For the next few days Edith and Michel communicated by telephone. By the weekend they were ready to be together again. They spent most of Saturday and Sunday in Michel's bed making love. They also drank wonderful wine, got slightly stoned, and ate gourmet meals which Michel prepared. Edith felt a little bit like a man as Michel puttered about the kitchen mumbling to himself about which ingredients to put into this or that. She sat and watched French television, hardly understanding a word, but not caring. Their time out of bed was mostly silent.

On Monday morning decisions had to be made.

"Should I move in tomorrow?"

"Why not tonight?"

"I'm having dinner with a producer and I don't

know how late I'll be."

"That's all right."

"I think tomorrow is better."

"Do what you want, Edith."

That sentence made Edith feel guilty; she would move in that night. Michel left for work and Edith made herself a second cup of coffee. She would send Sarah a note with her new address; she also wondered how she would get her bags up five flights of stairs when she could hardly get herself up. It meant having to call Michel at work to arrange for him to help her. She dreaded speaking with him again that day.

Edith did not move her luggage in that afternoon, but arrived at Michel's apartment late that night. The door was left open for her and Michel was already in bed. His voice called from the bedroom.

"You coming to me, or do I have to come to you?"

"I'll be right there."

Why had she decided to move in with him, to give up her independence? It was true, the apartment she had lived in was no longer available, but she knew that with a little more patience a new apartment could be found. Edith rationalized, telling herself that this would be a new experience. In truth, she was scared, and was allowing herself to be taken care of. In exchange, she would pretend to be an angel.

"You free me to come in touch with my fantasies."

Edith stroked Michel's hair as he spoke to her

in bed.

"I think I'm falling in love with you."

Edith remained silent. When she finally did speak, it was sadly and in a whisper.

"I'm afraid I don't know what love is."

Michel ignored her remark.

"Did you have a nice dinner with the producer?"

"Yes, very nice. He likes the script and was encouraging."

"Don't believe French producers. They all lie."

"I know, but I still enjoy being told my work is good."

"Of course you do, my darling."

Michel took Edith in his arms like a little girl. Edith's voice was weary.

"I'm tired tonight."

Michel didn't respond to her comment, but acknowledged it just the same by promptly going to sleep. Edith lay very still staring at the ceiling in the dark.

***

Edith noticed that her normal curiosity had come to a complete halt where Michel was concerned. For instance, he had a painting hanging over the right side of his bed covered with cellophane. It was impossible to see the painting through the cellophane, but Edith heard strange noises coming from inside it. She was afraid to ask Michel what the sounds were. Instead, she imagined a black widow spider hidden there. After two days of listening to the muted noise, Edith asked what it was.

"It's a wood worm. That painting is the only pornographic picture I've ever done and I wanted something alive in it."

Edith asked no more questions but continued to believe in her black widow spider theory. She dismissed the picture as something peculiarly German, but she didn't forget. When it became convenient for her to hate Michel, she would remember the picture and dismiss him as being slightly crazy. Best not to ask any more questions about the picture. Use it against him; he's vulnerable, even thinks I'm his angel. I hate his cooking.

Before dinner Edith and Michel were sitting on the floor of his apartment, sipping wine as usual.

"Does it make you tense having me here like this?"

"If it did, you wouldn't be here."

"How long have you been alone?"

"For three years. I decided after two seven-year relationships that failed not to be a conductor any more."

Edith realized that Michel spoke in metaphors half the time and she was about to get one now.

"I had become a train conductor and slowly realized I didn't know how to run the train, so I jumped off. Since jumping off, I don't know how to get back on. That's why I've been alone."

Edith felt moved by being able to understand him. It was as if they had some secret dialogue between them. She knew what it was, not to be able to get on the train. One had to risk being thrown off, either by death, separation, or joy for another human being. Best to let the train pass by and pity yourself for not getting aboard.

Michel spoke, "I'm making great efforts with you."

"Maybe that's what I'm feeling. Your efforts bring tension."

Again her mind snapped back to her mother. She too always seemed to be making efforts. Loving her children had not come easily. The tension of trying was unbearable. Mother and Michel were alike in many ways. Both quiet, withdrawn, aristocratic, and most comfortable when preparing a meal.

Edith remembered her feelings when she was alone in Michel's apartment for the first time. She had wanted to vomit. The smells from the bakery next door seemed to permeate the air, sickening her. When she looked around and saw the perfect order of things, she was overtaken by a desire to mess them, turn his drawers upside down, and smash his possessions. Edith clicked her mind back to the present, looked up at Michel, and spoke.

"Don't make such efforts, just try to enjoy me."

"But you're not real. This is all a dream."

"No, I'm sitting here next to you. Touch me; I'm real."

Michel refilled her glass with wine. "In a few

months you won't be real."

"Who knows?"

Michel changed the subject. "I bought string beans for a salad tonight. Why don't you help me cut them?"

Edith felt grateful being given something to do. She and Michel sat down at his work table to cut the beans.

"There's the string you have to pull down the middle."

"Why?"

"Otherwise it gets caught in your teeth and ruins the salad. Haven't you ever fixed fresh string beans before?"

"To tell you the truth, no." Edith's insides began to churn, producing rage. "I've better things to do with my time. Who gives a damn about some lousy string in a bean?"

Michel said nothing. When he finally spoke his words were measured.

"I think it's important to know these things."

"Well, I don't."

"Okay, Edith, it's all right."

She felt ashamed. Once more her mother's presence loomed before her. "I thought if I gave my children the right things to eat, it was enough. That was my way of giving. Forgive me for not loving you, but I never knew how."

***

"My grandfather committed suicide. My father never talked about it, but my mother told me."

They were eating the perfectly prepared bean salad. Every now and then, Michel would pointedly pull a string out from between his teeth. He continued his story.

"During the war, my father burned Nazi propaganda, but he never went underground, protested, or left the country. You see, he's a practical man and the only thing that mattered to him was his family. He couldn't afford ideals: making a living was the important thing. A very practical man."

"Are you ashamed?"

"I could never go back permanently. My home is now France. I even changed my name."

"What was it?"

"Helmut. Michel has the same meaning."

"Living in exile must be terrible."

"Not when it's voluntary."

"Forgive me for being so nasty about the beans. It wasn't personal. Sometimes I'm a bitch."

They finished eating and Edith began to clean up.

"Leave it, darling. I think we should go to bed."

Edith lay in Michel's arms with her eyes wide open, listening to the sounds of the wood worm, fearing it could kill her.

***

A week later, Edith was busy packing when she heard Michel enter the apartment.

She had been waking up each morning to acute feelings of anxiety and breathlessness. Conversation with Michel had become increasingly difficult and brought with it a tension she could no longer master. Edith decided it might be time for her to leave Paris.

"I'm in the bedroom."

Michel walked to the bedroom door and stood there, watching her.

"I'll be leaving for Florence tomorrow."

Michel remained calm, barely reacting to Edith's news.

"Did you get your ticket yet?"

"Yes, I picked it up at the train station today. It leaves tomorrow at four and gets in the next morning at nine."

Michel turned his back on Edith and made his way into the kitchen. His routine remained the same. Edith followed, feeling both guilty and relieved to be leaving. She sat down on the couch while Michel opened a fresh bottle of wine and poured it for them. His voice sounded flat when he spoke.

"You better finish your packing."

"I'm almost done. I can do the rest in the morning."

There was a thick silence between them. Edith felt betrayal in the air and had trouble breathing. They kept drinking. Neither spoke. Michel broke the silence first.

"On my way home from work tonight I met a

girl I know. She had just returned from San Tropez. When I asked her if she had had a good time, she lifted her skirt and showed me her pussy."

Edith's response was haughty and tight.

"What was that supposed to mean?"

"Well, I guess that she had a good time. It amused me."

For a moment Edith hated Michel, hated him for saying nothing about her departure and, instead, relating this stupid story.

"Sounds idiotic to me."

"She's just a friend."

Edith controlled her rage by remaining silent. What was the point? She'd be out of there tomorrow.

"If you need me, you'll call."

"Yes."

Edith and Michel were seated in a Vietnamese restaurant having dinner. Michel decided they should dine out for their last night together. He wanted to give Edith a treat. The restaurant was crowded with people who looked as if they had come there directly from work. Michel pointedly kept turning around to look at a blonde French working girl. Edith wished he would curse her for leaving, instead of playing spiteful games. These kinds of maneuvers always worked on her. The person had little to do with it. What mattered was the fairy tale. "Mirror, mirror on the wall, Who's the fairest of them all?"

Michel spoke lightly. "Maybe I'll surprise you and show up in Florence."

"I'd like that."

Edith lied again. She was leaving earlier than necessary to get away from feeling stifled, and yet felt compelled to say, "I'd like that." Had she used Michel and his convenient apartment to save money? If that were true, her guilt was justified. Somewhere it made her into a whore. Room and board in exchange for sex. Too simple. It had to be more complicated than that. Edith was attracted to Michel in some primitive way.

Back in the apartment they continued to drink and get stoned. Michel smoked a great deal. It usually made him impotent.

"So tomorrow you leave?" he asked. "Where will you stay when you return?"

Edith was waiting for this question, wondering when he'd ask.

"I don't know."

Michel's response came quickly. "I'll be in Germany, but you can stay here."

"I'd like that. Thank you."

"Well, it's settled then. You keep the key and I'll tell the concierge."

Edith felt unduly grateful for everything Michel did. She remembered similar feelings when her mother bought her a new dress.

"This is the last thing I'm getting you for the rest of the year."

"Yes, mother. Thank you, mother."

So grateful for a dress, an empty apartment. The

feelings came in waves; her head remained devoid of thoughts. She preferred being swept with the waves even though she risked drowning.

"Would you like to sleep now, my darling?"

Michel did not wait for a reply. He took Edith's hand and led her to the bedroom. Without speaking, they undressed and got into bed. Their love making was forced and never culminated in anything more than sleep. Edith knew that in the morning Michel would blame it on the grass. As he slept, she wondered if the sound coming from inside his pornographic picture might frighten her when she would be alone in his bed. She closed her eyes, waiting for sleep.

They were having breakfast. Edith was solicitous. Michel was all business.

"Would you like another cup of coffee?"

"No."

"Don't forget when you leave the apartment, return the key to the concierge, lock all the windows, and turn off the gas."

"I'll write it down."

"Good girl."

She wished he would go to work and stop giving instructions.

"I smoked too much last night. It's hard to remember anything."

There was nothing to remember.

Edith, being solicitous again, said, "You all right?" She wondered if Michel caught the insincerity in her voice.

"I'm fine."

He got up to leave and Edith walked him to the

door. They held each other for a moment.

"You have a good holiday, and call if you want me."

Edith nodded her head and closed the door after him. "You're my angel from the New World." Edith took a bath.

***

Sitting in her first-class compartment and looking out at the French countryside relaxed Edith and made her pensive. The conductor had tried holding her hand—he was probably wishing for some romance that night. She asked to be left alone. The movement of the train made her sleepy. She wondered if her energy was great enough to walk back the nine or ten cars it required to reach the dining car. Michel was slowly fading with the changing scenery.

Edith thought about Philippe, and how she had managed to see him again while staying with Michel. They had both made separate appointments for that particular evening.

"You're not always going to be here. I shouldn't give up all my lady friends. I'm just protecting myself, Edith, you understand."

She actually had understood, knowing well the value of insurance. She had her own in the person of Philippe, and called him in her hour of need.

They planned for dinner together, meeting at his apartment. She remembered how happy she had felt to be with him. His home was a complete mess. Treasures from exotic lands hung in haphazard fashion on the walls: poison arrows, naively painted pictures of saints, necklaces, purses, native costumes. What fun. So relaxed. Potato chips in the kitchen, no toilet paper for the bathroom, a jar of instant coffee in the living room, correspondence lying all over the desk. He helped her forget Michel and the sterility of his apartment, which seemed to anger her so much. Philippe's attitude was warm and friendly. Edith was like a prisoner pardoned for the night and enjoying her moments of freedom. It was that night that she had decided to leave Michel and go to Florence.

Edith and Philippe had gone to dinner in the student section of Paris. Edith felt beautiful and alive. Philippe really didn't want to know where she was staying, so it wasn't discussed. They acted as if they had been together always—a good dinner, easy conversation, affectionate glances. The restaurant was small and crowded, and yet a feeling of privacy existed between the two of them. He told her he was leaving for the South Sea Islands in a day or two, which only added to Edith's comfort.

She thought about that now, as she looked out the train window. All her life, commitments had been difficult. Everything was tenuous. Relationships, work, friendships, all had a way of making her uncomfortable. She never trusted any of it. Her love affairs were particularly disappointing. Edith wasted months trying to conquer someone she secretly despised. Once he was hers, hatred was all she could give. Her lovers had all been dismissed without explanation. Yet she felt no ill feelings for Philippe, who had given her nothing. Michel bore the brunt of her rage. Her memories moved to the rhythm of the train—kill, hate, fear—fear, hate, kill—hate, hate, hate—kill, kill, kill—fear, fear, fear.

She remembered Philippe had driven her back to Michel's apartment after they made love. She kissed him good night in the car and walked right into Michel entering the building at the same time. Laughingly Michel had put his arm around her, wanting to know if she had enjoyed her evening without him. They walked up the five flights of stairs arm in arm. Having just left Phillippe's bed helped relieve the tension with Michel. In fact, it had almost made her feel affection for him.

Edith began to get hungry. The thought of walking through the entire train to eat discouraged her from moving. "How silly, just get up and do it." As she made her way through the cars, her strength increased. The train felt like it was traveling at great speed. At first, Edith had trouble keeping her balance as she tried to slide the door of each car open. After a while it became fun. The French, the Italians, crowded the corridors as she pushed her way by. There were babies crying, mothers breast-feeding, people hanging out the windows breathing in the summer air. Life was pulsating out of these second-class cars. She was a stranger from a different world passing through. Everyone was polite to this lady who wasn't one of them. When she reached the dining car, starvation overtook her. She piled her tray with hot chicken, rolls, cheese, wine, and looked for a place to sit down. Edith spied an empty table and sat with her food. Why couldn't she sit next to someone, start a conversation? Terror invaded her. Everyone in the dining car had a yellow napkin but Edith. That meant having to leave her table to get one. She couldn't move.

"I need a yellow napkin. I *need* a yellow napkin."

She licked her fingers rather than expose herself to the eyes of the people in the dining car. A handsome man sitting alone stared at her. She ignored him. Maybe he was an Italian killer. One had to be safe traveling alone. The lights were too bright, reminding her of that first dinner with Michel. "If only I had my dark glasses." Her food was finished. The trip back to her compartment felt long and frightening. She lost her agility at opening doors. The people in the aisles became obstacles instead of friendly faces. In passing she glanced into one compartment only to meet the eyes of the staring man from the restaurant. Her pace quickened. She finally reached her haven, locked the door, took a sleeping pill, and went to bed with her clothes on.

***

Florence was hot. Edith went directly to her hotel and immediately fell asleep. Upon awakening, the heat of the city lured her from her air-conditioned room. Edith had always loved the heat. It was never too hot for her. She roamed the streets of Florence.

As the days passed, Edith roamed the streets of Florence. Each morning, she'd walk slowly across the Ponte Vecchio, absorbing her surroundings. As she moved from stall to stall on the lovely old bridge, looking at the jewelry, the antiques, what impressed her most was not what she saw but rather what she heard. It was the sound of the Italian language. She found it beautiful. It was like a song whose unknown words touched unknown feelings inside her. She was curious to see the faces of the people who made these wonderful sounds.

They were ordinary, full-featured Mediterranean faces. And they used their hands as well as their tongues to express sympathy, contempt, emphasis. Their liquid voices had a dynamic range from loud to soft that was seldom heard on the sidewalks of Manhattan. Edith really wasn't interested in the wares being sold but she loved the ambience. Strolling along the Ponte Vecchio, life felt peaceful, almost drowsy.

One day it was very hot and Edith decided to stop for a cold drink. She promised herself she'd return immediately to the Ponte Vecchio after her refreshment. There was a small outdoor cafe close to the bridge and she sat down at one of the tables. She lit a cigarette and watched the people walk by. It was hot and as she waited for her iced coffee, a smile crossed her face. Edith remembered her parents coming home from Florence with at least a dozen Florentine Zippo lighter holders. She could hear her father's voice exclaiming what great gifts they were. Now, fifteen years later, the exact same holders were being sold. It made Edith feel that Florence would go on forever. But today, she had no desire to buy anything. Just being there satisfied her.

Her drink arrived and she greedily gulped it down. The sun really was hot. The sweat poured down her face, which made her wonder how it might feel to be roasted alive. The image of Michel and her mother being put on skewers and going round and round over an open fire came to mind. The skewers went through them easily, as she imagined them hollow inside. When they were sufficiently burnt, Michel and her mother might make tasty eating.

What insane thoughts to be having in this most beautiful of all cities! Florence, a place that celebrates life. "What a relief to be gone from Michel." She paid her check and left the cafe. Her oppressive thoughts sent her back to the hotel.

Once in the room, she was still haunted by the image of Michel and her mother being burnt alive. Their cooking always made her want to vomit, gave her diarrhea. Vaginal juices, sperm coated their food.

As Edith lay on her bed, she heard her ten-year-old voice asking to sleep with her mother. "Yes." Edith wondered that no matter the hour, her mother had always been awake. Was she waiting for the call? Edith saw herself slowly getting out of bed and making that frightening trip down the hall to her mother's bedroom. Each step felt like a mile. Monsters were coming from the darkness trying to choke or stab her to death. When she finally reached her mother's bed, she cuddled into those outstretched arms for safety. She had made it down the hall of hell, and slept a deep, quiet sleep.

After barely a week, the heat of Florence was getting to her. Maybe it was time to return to Paris. "Michel will be gone by now," she thought. The more Edith considered it, the more she liked the idea.

***

Edith moaned her way up the five flights of stairs, suitcases in hand, to Michel's apartment. Walking into the apartment, Edith was struck again by its bizarre quality. Once she was relaxed, she became very aware of the pictures and objects surrounding her.

"What kind of art is this?" she said out loud.

She was referring to some candied mice that

Michel had encased in lucite and which was hanging on the kitchen wall. Edith shook her head and answered her own question.

"I don't know. I never want to know."

Edith sat blankly staring. Suddenly feeling a shortage of time, she began to snoop. She went through Michel's drawers looking at pictures of family, old girl friends, men friends, letters, clothes, anything he might have hidden. Edith found a woman's sweater and immediately took it, placing it in her suitcase. She found a snapshot of Michel's toe. The toe had nail polish on it.

"What in God's name is this?" she wondered.

Edith tried opening a closet only to find the door locked. She found the key in one of the desk drawers, and opened it. Everything looked normal enough. Camera equipment, winter coats, luggage, but underneath a pile of books she found some pornographic pictures. Leaving everything in place, she sat down on the couch to look at Michel's secret life: Women in black stockings tied and gagged; blindfolded women in the nude; women with women. Edith felt disappointed. She had expected richer, more bizarre fantasies from him.

"I'll put them back. He'll know if anything is out of place."

She returned the pictures to where they were found and relocked the closet door. Edith put the key in the desk.

Almost as an afterthought, Edith pulled open a drawer she had already gone through. She pulled out an embroidered baby's bib. Edith smiled, remembering Michel asking her if she wanted to see his most beautiful possession. She had expected a rare Moroccan treasure to appear. Instead he had shown her the bib. Edith put it back. A feeling of depression came over her. She wanted to leave the apartment. It was time for dinner anyway.

Once outside, Edith felt better. Her old fears disappeared. She saw the beauty of Paris through well-focused eyes. She wandered into an empty restaurant and sat down. As she waited for her food, she thought.

"I love this city and find it very beautiful, but I don't care if I never see it again. It's not my world.

"I don't know if my world is any place on earth. Maybe it's only in my head. I'm terrified of dying in New York or Paris. The earth wouldn't protect me."

She stopped thinking when the food was placed before her.

That night Edith went to bed early. She rolled over on her side only to see the outline of her figure in the low, horizontal mirror next to Michel's bed, and fell asleep.

It was six o'clock in the morning. Edith heard the front door open and close. She knew the anxious footsteps that walked quickly in and out of the bedroom. It was Michel and she pretended to be asleep. Edith continued to lie in bed, dreading Michel's presence. Why did he have to come back and ruin everything?

Michel stood in the doorway. Edith opened her eyes, feigning surprise. Michel's voice was cold. His body stood rigid and his tone was icy.

"I'll be leaving tonight. I'm driving with a friend to the south of France."

Edith chose to ignore his remark, not understanding his coldness. She moved herself out of bed and gave him a friendly hug. Edith knew Michel was hurt, but didn't know why. She spoke firmly to him.

"We can spend the day together."

They ate breakfast. Michel and Edith were seated face to face.

"I hope you're not too angry about my having gone to Florence."

"No."

Edith stood up and went into the bathroom, firmly locking the door behind her. She took a bath. When she got out, Michel was in bed waiting for her.

Their love making went deep. Edith felt Michel's penetration far inside her. She moved with it, holding nothing back. They were reaching for another level of ecstasy, knowing this was possibly their last time together. Edith's pleasure cried out from her, turning into real tears.

Michel held her.

"When you cry, I cry too."

He caressed her breasts, her vagina, licking her, loving her. Then with renewed force, he lunged inside her, giving her his very essence. They had exhausted themselves and lay very still. Michel spoke first.

"This time I'm leaving you. Last time you left me, but this time I'm leaving you."

Edith realized he hadn't forgiven her for going away. She was sad he had chosen this moment for revenge.

"Do you think you could live with me, Edith?"

How strange he was, swinging from spite to need.

"I don't know."

"We could live in Morocco or Italy, wherever you'd like."

"I don't know. I don't know."

Michel got out of bed and looked down at Edith's naked body.

"You were supposed to be my angel from the New World."

He left the room to make some tea.

***

The summer had been a mixed time for John. On the one hand he enjoyed a beautiful house in South Hampton where he spent his weekends entertaining guests and playing tennis. John received much gratification when he was complimented on the splendor of his home. He knew Edith would hate it as she had always refused to go to the Hamptons, she preferred the Berkshires. Yet it gnawed at him whenever he thought of her traveling about Europe and what she might be doing.

At these moments, he was grateful to have his dog, Gino, next to him. John had always thought of Edith as something of a gypsy and was both pained and excited when he'd picture her with other men. She had not written to him once and this also bothered him. Realistically he knew he had no right to expect otherwise, but there it was just the same. His mistress was probably being unfaithful and he didn't like it. These thoughts, coupled with the fact that he really did miss Edith, spurred him on to call Sarah more and more frequently.

How anticlimactic it all was! Sarah had taken a job and was no longer at home during the day. How was John to know she was earning $309 a week and having a flirtation with her boss? After putting himself through this kind of torture for a few weeks, John finally realized she was either away or working. He would have to try her at night. This was always more risky, but he had few choices.

It was three o'clock in the morning. John made his way into his den, walking through the darkness. He was praying Sarah was in the city and that she'd be the one to answer the phone. He sat down on the couch. The phone was facing him on a coffee table. He thought about the table and how it had cost him three thousand dollars. Suddenly he was annoyed with himself for having spent so much money on a piece of furniture. He did not feel nervous any more about his call.

Somehow his mission seemed more appropriate in the dark than in broad daylight. If Paul answered, he could always hang up. John lit a cigarette and picked up the receiver. He dialed and waited.

"Hello."

Thank God, it was Sarah. He wanted to curse at her, scream, threaten her, but instead hung up the phone and continued to think about his coffee table. He touched it with his hand to feel the smooth marble surface. John sat wondering why it was that he had to live in such splendor. It made him a slave to his work, which he was beginning to hate. But he loved possessions. They kept him busy in his spare time. He was either buying them or returning them. First it was African art, then Indian art, then antique furniture. Each possession was a responsibilty gradually weighing him down like a relationship. He began to hate the beautiful coffee table that had to be polished and cared for every day. If it was neglected, he became furious, reminding his maid of what it had cost him. But if he never bought these precious things he'd not have to worry about them.

"There's something nice about traveling light," Edith used to say. He wished he knew how. John smoked another cigarette and looked at the New York skyline from his den windows. That was another thing he had to have.

"I can't move into any apartment without a view," he had told Edith. So he had his precious view, but his happiest moments were with Edith in her small apartment. John felt a tinge of self-disgust and went back to bed. He was content that Sarah was in town. He'd call her another time when he wasn't so preoccupied.

***

Sarah hadn't seen very much of Nicholas over the summer. He'd gone to California for a few weeks to put up a piece of sculpture and had only just returned. When she received her aborted, 3 A.M. phone call, she was sure it was him. She couldn't believe that John would ever find the nerve to call her again. Her feelings were mixed. She and Paul had been quiet together and getting on. Her job was providing her with a little money and a flirtation. She was not discontent until the moment of the call. Then her thoughts and sexuality ran back to Nicholas. The old longings returned. Memories in the dark. Nicholas looking at her and asking what kind of games she liked when they made love.

"No games."

"That must be very boring. Will you play my games?"

Sarah had answered with a shit-eating grin on her face, "I'll do whatever you want."

"I'd like to tie you up and tease you. Would you like that?"

"That would excite me."

Nicholas had gotten up from the bed.

"There's some rope in my closet. I'll get it."

While Nicholas was out of the room Sarah undressed. Nicholas returned with the rope and proceeded to tie her hands to the bedposts and her ankles to the foot of the bed. He started with her lips and licked his way down to her vagina. His tongue moved in and out of her like a snake. Sarah wanted to move but couldn't, which only added to her excitement. Nicholas felt her heat and entered her. He came quickly and Sarah was disappointed. When it was over she remembered feeling rather silly tied to his bed.

"Please untie me now."

Nicholas obeyed. Sarah got dressed and returned home to her husband. In retrospect Sarah just remembered the excitement and desired it again.

"Maybe he'll call tomorrow," she whispered to herself as she returned to sleep.

***

Sarah's editing skills were improving. David Marin was a good teacher and gave her responsibility. They worked well together and he was the first boss that Sarah didn't resent. Every now and then she caught him whistling "That's why the lady is a tramp" and became paranoid, convinced he knew of her unfaithfulness, but nothing was ever said and their days were spent in work and friendly flirting. Sarah didn't understand why she felt so little resentment at his orders. In previous jobs she couldn't stand being the underling and being told what to do. She'd find herself shaking with rage when asked to do her job. It made her feel like a dog. She'd either quit, cry, or have a tantrum, which invariably led to her almost always being jobless.

But this summer, it was working, maybe because Nicholas was away and she was grateful to have a place to go every day, or perhaps her attraction to David was sustaining her. Either way she was learning and her mind was distracted from Paul and Nicholas. But the phone call had rekindled her desires. Poor Sarah felt hooked again.

"I wish Edith were here."

Her old furies began to surface against her superior. She wanted to be with Nicholas, not stuck in some grubby editing room with a married man. Besides, his wife kept visiting them, accompanied by their six-year-old daughter. It reminded her of her childless state and the fact that if she didn't get pregnant soon, it might be too late. This thought threw her into great despair but she didn't want Paul's child, only Nicholas's. Yet she still felt powerless to move. Sarah insisted on torturing herself when all she had to do to have everything she wanted was merely to walk out the door and not return.

The phone call of the night before was making her nervous. She couldn't wait to get home, making her lack of concentration on work obvious. David was annoyed with Sarah and once more she felt she was at one place but wished to be somewhere else. At the end of the day she rushed home from work, barely saying good-bye to David, to await her magic phone call. Upon returning to her loft she found a letter from Edith. She opened it with curiosity, wondering how her friend was surviving in Paris.

Dearest Sarah,

A belated Happy Birthday. I hope it was a good one. Did you receive my telegram? How are you feeling? I think of you often and wonder how your life is going. My address is on the back of the envelope if you feel like writing.

Love,
Edith

Sarah knew from this short note that Edith still hadn't quite forgiven her. She sat down and wrote her a letter, hoping in that way to make amends.

Edith had been home for ten days and hoped she could resist seeing John. She felt her trip had changed her but she wasn't sure how. She had just received a letter from Michel. She opened it with curiosity, not knowing what to expect.

> Edith darling,
>
> What's the problem with your parents? This is Michel speaking, from Paris, you remember. Do you want to make love or kill-kill pa and mum? Crazy idea—take a vacation with them. They love you, so much, so dearly, just accept—now that I thought you are prepared, open to accept. Take care and advantage of your dearest ones before they are gone—please. I gave you a surplus of affection, now you must be rich, if you understood me soul and body, little selfish, doting, spoiled child.

Edith put the letter down for a moment. She didn't understand what all the references to "pa and mum" were about. She had written him upon her return to New York, saying she was having some problems with her parents. They had entered her apartment when she was away and thrown out some of her possessions because they were either broken, old, or dirty. Edith had been furious and had mentioned her anger in her letter to Michel.

She picked up the letter again and began to read where she'd left off.

> Wake up, reddish witch, concentrate, your German shepherd is speaking. Work is work, love is luv, so don't mix toughness

and luv, be humble. Tonight is Yom Kippur which means New Year's and Redemption. As I'm more Moslem than Lutheran, we are celebrating tonight, brothers to sisters, so let it go, in its proper place. Look at yourself, my darling, do you really want to go into trouble with them? Shit—stop it. Please, for the sake of love, stop being so selfish. Start flying, be high, all the time with mum and dad—be a child, be a baby. Billie Holiday says: I'll be around, no matter how you treat me now, I'll be around, good-bye again, just now and then. Edith, I almost killed myself on the 20th of August, 6 A.M., the day you were supposed to leave Paris. Fortunately, a good friend from Berlin was with me. The car fell down the hill and landed upside down. My friend wasn't hurt at all. I broke a bone in my right arm and couldn't move it for twenty days. Anyway, we were very lucky. But the holidays became quite calm and morbid, because Catherine declared her love for me.

Edith once more put down the letter. It rested in her lap as she stared into space. "Who the hell is Catherine," she wondered. "He really sounds mad." Her eyes moved downward to the letter. She continued to read it.

As I was very pleased and annoyed, I struggled to do my best—without letting down my love for her man—a dear friend of mine. As I was traveling with my friend from Germany and the supernurse, who saved my poor arm in the accident, I went back to Paris, found your matches and note, and fell in love two days later.

Edith remembered leaving him matches from the French cinematique, the ones with movie stills on them. The note she had left him was a simple thank you.

I must thank you, my supernurse, and Cathy. You opened my heart and mind, so I could fall in love again. You gave me supreme confidence through fucking, pardon, making love, which I never found before. AS YOU CAME TO ME ON MY BIRTHDAY, YOU DID NOT COME TO KILL ME. But I did not want to kill myself after all, so what happened accidentally? My shoulder is still hurting and I'm now very careful. I hope you will find a director for your script. Saw *Shampoo* and *Day of the Locust,* both were deceiving, but that's the industry, a pain in the ass. I never fucked your ass, because the base of our affection was much too much, and I'm not supposed to hurt you. You understand, even if I have found true love, new love, twenty-five years old, boy's body, super brains. I really hope to see you soon, as we will move to New York soon. She wants to be in Manhattan for career and excitement. Why not? After all, moving keeps you young. Edith, I'm full of confidence, I never felt better, thanks to you and sisters. I'm beautiful, strong, and wise. I hope you will not let me down. We will meet again, maybe in New York City on my way west-east. I'm on the road, darling, and it's so nice, you can't imagine. The lady is a tramp, please keep moving.

I love you affectionately—Michel.

Edith picked up the letter.

"AS YOU CAME TO ME ON MY BIRTHDAY, YOU DID NOT COME TO KILL ME."

Why didn't she feel anything? No compassion for a man gone mad, a man she had lived with for two weeks in Paris. He had taken her in when she needed a place to stay, cooked for her every night, shared his mind and body with her. He had almost died, was going crazy, and she felt nothing. Edith didn't connect to the letter. After reading it again, a feeling of anger crept through her. She would write back and express her disappointment in him, call him weak. Excitement filled her body as a cruel letter began to shape itself inside her head.

Instead she thought of John, his betrayal, and the strumpet role she had played with him. This threw her into conflict. But as if some uncontrollable force was guiding her, she found her fingers dialing his number. It was almost as if her hands had separated from her body. She watched herself make the call as one might observe a stranger.

Edith called him on his private line, hoping to avoid his nosy secretary.

"Hello John."

"Edith! When did you get home?"

His voice was nervous but he sounded genuinely happy to hear from her. This warmed Edith and suddenly she wanted to see him. She lied when she answered his question.

"I just got home yesterday."

"Did you bring me a gift from Paris?"

"Uh-huh."

Another lie. Edith had spent all her money on herself and never could buy anything for John. It wasn't that she didn't think of it. But each time she thought of it she refused to buy it. Now she'd have to go to some Fifth Avenue store and get something from France to give him.

"Do you want to come to my apartment tomorrow?"

"Sure. What time?"

John thought a moment.

"How about twelve? I'll take a long lunch hour."

"Okay. I'll see you tomorrow."

Edith hung up the phone insulted that John had not insisted on seeing her that very moment.

Edith arrived for her rendezvous on time. She used the key John had given her. John was in bed waiting for her.

Edith immediately undressed and slipped into

bed next to him. John didn't speak, kiss, or caress Edith, he fucked her and came. When it was over the only sound Edith could hear was a song, "Sometimes I feel like a motherless child." It echoed through her head over and over. John spoke.

"Sorry to be so selfish, but I really needed that."

"Sometimes I feel like a motherless child," she thought.

"I missed you, Edith, and was afraid of losing you. I need you with me to keep on the right track."

"Sometimes I feel like I'm almost gone. Sometimes I feel like I'm almost gone. Sometimes I feel like I'm almost gone, a long way from home."

"Were you faithful to me when you were away?"

"No."

"Don't tell me about it."

"I won't."

"Sometimes I feel like a motherless child." There it went again. Edith couldn't get rid of the song. It was beginning to hurt her. She wanted to ease the pain. She took John's hand and placed it on her vagina.

"Satisfy me."

John obliged, and the song stopped.

They parted, but not before Edith had given John his gift from Saks. It was a sweater with the label "Made in France" written in French. They planned to see each other again in two days. Edith felt sad as she sat on the bus going home. She put on her dark glasses to avoid seeing or being seen. An image of Michel came to her. She saw herself lift her glass of wine.

"A toast to your birthday. I think we should drink to angels."

Michel clicked his glass to Edith's.

"To angels. Do you think you could see one with your dark glasses on?"

"Maybe."

Edith got off the bus, went directly to her apartment, and fell asleep.

Sarah was deeply depressed. Nicholas had called after a long period of time to tell her of his mother's death. He said she woke up one morning and walked into the Pacific Ocean without looking back. Nicholas was flying to California for her cremation. His father wanted her ashes scattered on the ocean.

Sarah had been unable to console her lover. Paul was present, preventing conversation. She found it odd that both she and Nicholas had lost their mothers through suicide and felt very close to him. Now he was as much an outcast as she was. She felt guilty about not being accessible to him in his hour of need. That would just about finish them forever, she thought. An image of a woman walking into the ocean formed itself in Sarah's head. Somehow she couldn't help feeling that it was a very poetic way to die.

***

After Nicholas returned from California, Sarah went to see him. He had just gotten back from his mother's funeral. The two of them sat in his loft together. Sex was no longer possible between them. He felt too betrayed and she too humiliated. Nicholas tried to be civil with this woman who had promised one day to be his wife. He rationalized his anger toward her, taking the blame on himself for having believed her. She was paralyzed, as paralyzed as his own mother had been. Sarah's mother had probably been paralyzed too. Why had he insisted on believing her lies and false promises? His mother's death had clarified that for him. He had wished to change Sarah, force movement, make an unloving woman love. As he had watched his mother's ashes being thrown into the ocean, he had realized he'd wished to do the same thing for his mother.

Why couldn't she have loved me, at least enough to stay alive? Even though he was now a man in his mid thirties, her suicide affected him as if he was still a child. She'd always been a depressed woman. Nicholas had spent his childhood yelling at her, abusing her, saying anything to elicit a response. He had done the same with Sarah but was now too tired to fight for her any longer. He spoke to Sarah in quiet tones.

"I realized there was no place for me in your life when you wouldn't leave Paul to come to me at the time of my mother's death."

"I'm so sorry Nicholas. I guess I've failed everyone."

"Most of all yourself. You'll never have a child

or really be a filmmaker. You'll lead Paul's life and someday he'll walk out on you too."

Sarah was contrite.

"I know. It's strange that both our mothers were suicides. It makes me feel very close to you."

"Not close enough to have come to me when I needed you."

His words stung her.

"Won't you give me one more chance? I'll leave Paul, I promise I will."

"Sarah, you've been saying that for two years and I've wanted to believe you. I tried to shake you in every possible way. You're immovable and stuck. Please don't call anymore or speak to me if we meet on the street. I really want you out of my life."

Sarah looked at him pleadingly but this time she knew he was serious. What more was there to say? She left his loft and returned home.

Thank God Edith is back in the country, Sarah thought. She quickly dialed her friend's number.

"I'm in such a panic, Edith. This time he meant it. I called him as soon as I got home and he hung up on me."

Sarah was hoping Edith might relieve some of the anxiety. Edith's voice was resigned.

"Sarah, you've told me this same story a hundred times. He always takes you back. Why should it be different now?"

"His mother's suicide and my not going to him

right away. It's serious. He realizes I'm not even a friend."

Edith was silent for a moment before answering.

"Maybe you're right. It might also be the best thing. You couldn't leave Paul with Nicholas waiting. It seemed to make you feel too guilty. Now you have the possibility of doing something for yourself, just for yourself."

"I know you're right, but I feel a terrible loss. The only thing I want to do is speak to him, walk the streets and find him. It's so creepy."

"It reminds me of when we were in high school and used to follow the boys home hoping they would talk to us," Edith said.

"Edith, I'm afraid to leave the house in case he calls. I blame Paul for depriving me of the life I want with Nicholas. The only thing I can do is sleep."

"I think you've got to fight for yourself now, Sarah. The best thing would be to find some work."

"I know. I'm up for a few editing jobs. Let's hope I get one. I don't think I'll ever finish my film. It's so unclear and empty."

"Well, anytime you want me to look at it, let me know."

"Thanks, Edith."

Sarah put down the phone and took a good look around her loft. It occurred to her that she had never really taken in her surroundings. She saw how empty her home really was. It made her feel so sad.

She began to water her plants. She even spoke to

them. Suddenly they seemed so lonely in her large empty loft that she felt sorry for them.

"How are you today, my sweet ferns, and you, my lovely palm?"

When Sarah heard the sound of her own voice, she felt like an idiot. She finished watering the rest of the plants in silence.

She then began rummaging through her closets. She found two beautiful tapestries which she'd forgotten she owned. One was a patchwork quilt made from different silk ties. The shapes and colors were playful, lively; they almost danced. The other tapestry was more serious, a creamy white cotton interspersed with clusters of blue birds. Sarah also found some hammered plates of Turkish copper and two hand-painted pottery vases. The feeling that these things were hers connected her to them. They felt like extensions of herself and she suddenly didn't want them hidden away in the closet any longer.

She laid the tapestries on the floor, straightening them where they were crooked. "Why am I doing this," she thought. "Let them lie naturally." She placed her plates and vases here and there, looked at them and moved everything again and again until she was satisfied. Sarah was working herself into a real sweat. She could feel herself perspiring as she moved the objects from place to place. She finally got tired and walked to her bed, wondering what had precipitated this burst of energy, but couldn't come up with any profound answer.

"Just change for change's sake," she said aloud.

As her eyes closed she hoped Paul would like what she had done to their barren home.

Edith hung up the phone and wondered at the ease with which she gave advice. She still hadn't liberated herself from John. The external circumstances of her life were gradually changing but she remained a coward. Once my short story is published, everything will fall into place, she rationalized. Secretly she knew it wasn't true. She had to free herself of all links with the past and the surrogates she used in their place. It was a difficult task, but little stirrings inside her were beginning to take place. Sometimes it was a moment, then a whole minute that Edith knew the feeling of being an adult. She liked herself best at those times. The first step was to leave John, the rest would follow.

***

John stopped calling Edith as often, hoping she'd come to her senses. Her insubordination was becoming impossible. He found her tone on the telephone flip and she was almost always too busy to see him. Their sex lacked its usual sensuality as Edith became more and more silent while making love. She had always stimulated John with rich fantasies, making him feel like a king. Edith had previously called herself his private whore and described imaginary orgies to him which included other men and women. Now she hardly spoke.

John was afraid of becoming impotent once more. His anger toward Edith, at least, was sustaining his erections. Their relationship had become a contest of wills. Edith was trying to castrate him with her coldness. He'd fight her to the end.

"It's always so sexy to be with you."

John was stroking Edith's breast and talking at the same time. They were spending the night together. As John tried to arouse her, Edith's mind drifted.

"I don't know what I'm doing here with this man. He and my best friend are talking filth to one another on the telephone. I wonder if I'll ever tell him I know. I really loathe him."

Suddenly Edith's hate turned to excitement. She looked up at John and spoke.

"Let's jerk off together."

John was pleased. They sat up facing one another. John placed his hand on his cock and rubbed it up and down. Edith, leaning on one arm, placed her fingers inside her vagina and moved them back and forth. Every now and then she'd stop and grab John's cock with her hand. This excited him. John finally came. Edith didn't, but stopped her motions just the same. She and John went under the covers to sleep. John placed his arms around Edith's naked body. Edith felt sick and wanted to go home. Instead she said nothing and pretended to sleep. John whispered in her ear.

"You're like a mother, sister, lover, and whore all in one. It's perfect."

Edith remained silent. She was forgetting how to smile magnificently or say thank you insincerely. Her silence had become her new weapon and she used it now.

***

Sarah found a job editing Playtex Living Bra commercials. Her salary was $600 a week, which she was very proud of. She and Nicholas were no longer speaking. They had passed each other on the street a few times and he hadn't even acknowledged her. The salary eased some of the pain but not all of it.

Paul told her he no longer wanted a child because of their loveless life together. He liked the changes she'd made in the loft but said it was all too late. The salary eased some of the pain but not all of it.

Edith informed her she was a lousy friend because of her self-absorption. The salary eased some of the pain but not all of it.

The work she was doing was unfulfilling and tedious. She'd go home at night and fall right to sleep. The phone calls had ceased so there was nothing to stay awake for. If it wasn't for that $600 a week there would be little to look forward to. Sarah was finding pleasure in watching her bank account grow. Soon she'd accumulate more money than Paul. That thought comforted her.

Since her affair with Nicholas, she and Paul paid their own way. If they went out for dinner together, each paid separately. They borrowed money from one another, making it legal with IOU notes. Sex hadn't occurred between them for a year. Still they remained together. There was no reason for them to remain married but they seemed glued for life. Occasionally Paul turned the kitchen table over in a rage but it was soon forgotten and life went on as usual.

Edith often asked Sarah if Paul was having affairs. Sarah's reply was that she didn't know and didn't care. As long as she could make money and sleep, what Paul was doing in his spare time didn't interest her. Sarah's dreams of becoming, or being with, the *artiste extraordinaire* had evaporated with the disappearance of Nicholas. Playtex Living Bra commercials had replaced all that.

Sarah was getting more and more work. When the Playtex commercial was finished, she went right to work on another job. This one was a bit better. It was a half hour television pilot. Again she'd be making a lot of money. This time she'd even have an assistant. Edith asked her how it felt to be the boss.

"I'm sorry for my assistant. It feels ridiculous giving orders. When I was an assistant I couldn't stand it, and now that I'm in charge I still can't stand it."

She and Edith both laughed.

Sarah loved the money she was earning, but when she looked into the other editing rooms and saw that all the editors were female, she felt her life had become very ordinary. Sarah worked all day and went home to Paul. They were civil to one another, and seemed resigned to each other. They'd have dinner, make small talk, and then go off to sleep. Life had become very quiet, dead.

Paul was satisfied that his wife's affair was finished. To the world, he had won. Now, in a strange turn of events, he thought about leaving her. But he also enjoyed their quiet life and Sarah's passivity. Paul was more ambitious than he'd realized and didn't like distractions from his work. Even sex was a distraction, therefore Sarah's lack of warmth was acceptable. As a substitute, he took to masturbating in the bathroom at least three times a week. One night, Sarah and Paul discussed their platonic relationship. She began.

"Are you having an affair?"

"No."

"What do you do for sex?"

"I masturbate. Don't you?"

"No."

"I can't believe it. You do nothing?"

"That's right."

"Doesn't seem normal to me."

"It's not."

"Poor Sarah. It must be awful never to get it off."

"Right now sex repulses me."

"Didn't it always?"

"Maybe. I don't know."

Sarah thought about Nicholas and how she had desired him. At the moment it all sickened her. Hiding in a dark editing room by day and sleeping at night was what she wanted. No more hysterics, waiting for phone calls, being poor. She and Paul probably lived like most married couples. It was a relief. Occasionally they'd have friends over for dinner or spend a weekend in the country, but there was no meaning in what they did. Only Nicholas and his force had been able to move Sarah, but apparently not enough.

Sarah no longer felt depressed or frightened. Instead everything she saw or touched looked gray. Bright lights and subtle shades were all the same to her. Even her beautiful green eyes turned gray when she stared at her reflection in the mirror. She no longer thought about having children. She was too tired and couldn't think of an acceptable father.

> *I saw a woman playing in the water with her two children and the sight of her made my heart go out.*

Sarah remembered her letter to Edith.

***

Edith looked at John from across the table. They were having dinner together. John was explaining some new tricks he'd taught his dog. Edith couldn't believe he was really as stupid as he sounded. In reality, he wasn't.

John sensed Edith's coldness and knew what she wanted to say. He didn't want to hear it so he told dog stories. Edith never gave him any credit for insight. She thought she had a monopoly on it. In truth, John was always on to her. That's the main reason he never seriously thought of marrying her. Finally John stopped talking. Edith began.

"I think we should separate."

John said nothing and continued eating. Edith went on.

"I think we're both asking for too little for ourselves by staying together. It's not you, it's me. Another kind of woman could probably make you much happier."

"What a coward," John thought. "She's trying to spare my feelings."

"It's not that I don't love it in bed. You know I do. That will be hard to give up."

She was bullshitting him, knowing how frightened he was of impotence.

"Edith, do what you want. I won't bother you anymore if you don't want me to."

His response frightened her. He was being so nice. Was she making a mistake?

"Thank you, John. I love you." And for that moment, she did.

John felt bad when he got home that night. Life without Edith seemed barren. Thank God he had his dog. But even Gino's affection didn't ease the empty feeling. He wasn't sure if he loved Edith or was afraid for himself. He lay down on his living room couch. The thought of going into his bedroom depressed him. He wondered how long he'd have to go without sex. Gino stared at him with his longing brown eyes.

John patted the dog's head and opened the fly of his pants. He took out his penis and began to masturbate. Gino sat silently beside his master. With one hand John continued to stroke his dog's head. His other hand brought relief. His sperm covered the dog. John lay perfectly still for many minutes. He then lifted Gino and took him into the bathroom. The hour was late, but his dog needed a bath.

John's days were growing long. He missed Edith. There were always other women to flirt with but they disgusted him. On one occasion he allowed himself to go back to a woman's apartment. She'd been introduced through a friend. They began to undress. She went into the bathroom. John went in after she returned to her bed. He jumped when he saw two false teeth swimming in a glass of water. He quickly left the bathroom, dressed, and went home.

He wondered what Edith was doing and wished he was with her. Life was closing in on him and he knew it. He'd known for a long time but avoided it when he had Edith. Once more he wanted to call

Sarah, and hurl his vulgarity through the telephone lines. This no longer seemed possible. John realized that Sarah knew he'd been the one calling her.

"She has as much to be ashamed of as I do."

That was his thinking but he couldn't stop his hands from trembling everytime he thought about it. If Sarah knew, Edith knew. They would think him pathetic, maybe laugh at him. John remembered how Edith had suddenly left for Europe after his last call to Sarah. Sarah had said, "I think I know who this is."

That cunt, thought John. Why didn't she just say, "I know who this is?" Or, even better, why didn't she say his name and get it all out in the open? Those two were a pair of sneaks. Good riddance to them.

These thoughts were intolerable but a martini or two relieved the pain. He found it impossible to have sex with anyone, including himself. Many an afternoon he sat in his office with a drink in one hand, stroking his dog with the other. All his manic energy seemed to be drained from him. Money, work, possessions were quickly losing the joy they had once brought him. He'd become an empty shell and all the food in the world couldn't fill him. In fact, most of the time he felt starved.

His partner was becoming disgusted and John thought about buying him out. Then he'd have to work. The more he thought about it, the better he liked the idea. What a challenge! Give his partner all his money and start from scratch. He'd show them. What a purpose. Most people couldn't make one million dollars in a lifetime. He'd make two. Even Edith would have to be impressed with that. He'd speak to his partner, his lawyer, and begin negotiations. No more afternoon drinks or remorse over dead romances. It was time to make that second million.

John once more found a reason to live. He had never tired of impressing the world. "I'll call Edith to tell her of my plans," he thought. "She'd never hang up on me."

Edith quickly picked up the ringing telephone.

"Hi, Edith."

For a moment she didn't recognize John's voice. He was the last person she'd expected to hear from. Her voice took on a cold and formal tone.

"Hello, John. How are you?"

"Great, and getting better all the time."

"Sounds good."

Total silence followed between them. Edith wasn't going to make this easy for him.

"Have you been writing?"

"A little."

"How's Sarah?"

"Fine."

This conversation with John was making Edith feel that her life was going backward. She knew he wanted to tell her something and waited.

"I've decided to buy out my partner, which will leave me broke."

"That's very courageous of you. What will you do for money?"

"I'll still have my yearly salary. It just means all my savings will be gone. I'm going to start all over and see what I can do on my own."

Poor John, thought Edith. He'll only have his $100,000 a year salary to live on. Edith suspected that John's partner no longer adored John the way he needed to be adored.

"Don't you ever want to stop making money and do other things for yourself?"

John detected the contempt in Edith's voice.

"You certainly never minded when I spent it on you."

"You're right, but you don't spend it on me any more and never will again."

"I see it's impossible for you to ever feel happy for me."

"That's right. Your dreams make me sad; not happy, sad."

"I'll never bother you again, Edith."

"Please don't, and try not to bother Sarah either."

John was caught off guard. He had never realized what a dirty fighter Edith was. He said nothing and hung up the phone in a rage. As he sat at his desk he looked down at his hands. They were clenched into fists. Slowly he released his fingers. His face was red with fury. A drink. He wanted a drink.

John made himself a martini from his office liquor cabinet. He buzzed his secretary, telling her to take all messages. He was available to no one, not even his partner. He then proceeded to get drunk. John's head reeled with Edith's words.

"Don't bother me and try not to bother Sarah either."

Why wasn't she impressed with his money? Instinctively he felt it was because he was a rotten lover. John really wanted to blow his brains out but he didn't have a gun. He finally fell asleep at his office desk and didn't wake up until morning. Upon awakening he felt better and went home to shower and shave. There was no one to greet him or ask where he'd been all night. Fucking pig, cunt Edith, he thought as he jumped into an ice cold shower.

***

John had grown to despise Edith. He hoped each day that she would need something. Money, sex, anything. He wanted the opportunity to say no and turn her down cold. His impotence appeared as a mild inconvenience next to his rage toward Edith. His plans to buy his partner out had succeeded but the thrill he expected to feel never materialized. Making money came easily to John and it no longer excited him. He felt hemmed in, enclosed, and looked forward to traveling.

He had to go to Colorado on business. Maybe he'd get lucky and meet a cute stewardess on the plane. John knew from experience she'd speak nicely to him and make him feel good. They were trained to behave like that, but he didn't care. A trained woman was better than a nasty gypsy like

Edith. He then realized why he loved his dog so much. Gino was trained and would remain that way. The women he knew dared to change and challenge him. For a split second he thought he might take his dog out west with him. No, the stewardess would do just fine.

***

Sarah picked up Edith in her brother's rickety old Volkswagen. One of the front headlights was missing and Edith had little faith in its staying power. Sarah had insisted on the two of them having lunch in Weehawken, New Jersey.

"We'll eat overlooking the water. It's nice there."

Edith had always liked a ride in a car, so she didn't object. She had forgotten how funky Sarah's car was.

"I hope this can get us there and back," said Edith as she got into the front seat.

"No problem."

They sputtered their way to New Jersey and Edith was surprised to find herself seated in a pleasant restaurant overlooking the water. It faced Grant's tomb. Edith looked at her friend and was startled by her beauty, as if seeing her for the first time.

"You look wonderful, Sarah."

Sarah smiled self-consciously.

"Do I? I always feel my head is too large."

"What are you talking about?" Edith was puzzled by Sarah's confession.

"You mean to say I've never discussed this with you before?"

Edith shook her head.

"That's one of the reasons I've stayed with Paul. We're both large and have big heads. I don't feel like a freak with him."

Edith was amazed.

"Don't you know you're beautiful? Everyone tells you what a beauty you are."

"I know. That doesn't matter so much to me any more. The important thing now is accomplishment. But I still think my face is enormous, which makes me self-conscious. Nicholas was my height. Sometimes I felt grotesque next to him."

Edith looked at her friend, at her lovely green eyes, at her hair that was always tousled, as if she'd just washed it and forgot to comb it. She felt a surge of love for her childhood friend and no longer was angry at her for past betrayals.

"I love you, Sarah."

Sarah smiled at her friend and spoke.

"In spite of everything, we're improving with age, aren't we, Edith?"

"I hope so."

***

Sarah and Paul were having an unusually quiet dinner. Sarah knew something was on Paul's mind and was patiently waiting to hear what it was. Sarah had been using Paul's assistant Kate to help edit the television pilot she was presently working on. There were times when Sarah wondered about her. She would lose her temper easily and lash out at Sarah in an inappropriate manner. Sarah had just finished telling Paul her feelings on the subject, when he lapsed into total silence. Silence. What a strange phenomenon it was. It was sometimes louder than the loudest shout in the world. Paul's silence fell on Sarah like a dead weight. Words. Here they come.

"Kate and I are having an affair."

Paul's words stung Sarah, but his silence had prepared her.

"How long?"

"Since she worked with me on my film."

"You mean it was going on in my house and under my nose? Then you had the nerve to recommend that she work with me?"

"When I did that, I thought it was over with her."

"This wipes the slate clean. We're even now."

Paul looked at his wife.

"You're right, we're even now."

Sarah left the table. She felt curiously calm as she sat down on her bed to think. She was almost forty years old. The man she loved was gone. Her husband was probably in love with another woman. And she was childless. Her work was the one positive element in her life. Why wasn't she more panicked, furious?

It was curious, but her overriding emotion was one of relief. This may have been the moment she'd been waiting for. It might put an end to the drifting and force decisions long overdue. Paul walked over to the bed and sat down beside her. He put his arm around her as he spoke.

"Kate and I were both sex starved. You haven't slept with me in a year. It was bound to happen sooner or later."

"All those fucking nights she had dinner here." Sarah snapped, the rage surfacing. "You must have felt like a real king having us both waiting on you."

Paul was pleased by his wife's jealousy.

"I did," he said.

Sarah slapped his face.

"You better watch it, Sarah. After your tawdry affair of two years, I'd suggest you keep your mouth shut."

Sarah knew he was right and gently touched her husband's face on the spot she had slapped. Her head nestled close to his.

"I guess we're going to have to make some serious decisions."

Paul took his wife in his arms.

"I need time alone with Kate. I want to know if I love her."

Sarah understood.

"I'll go to California for three weeks and stay at the Zen Center. It will be good for me to do some work with roshi. That way we'll both have time and distance to think," Sarah said.

They held each other like two sad friends.

"I should leave next week; my job will be finished by then."

"All right."

The slate was clean and Sarah was finally free to choose the direction of her life. Their week together was quiet and subdued. Paul openly went out with Kate one night, leaving Sarah alone.

"Can't you even wait till I'm out of town?"

Paul didn't see anything wrong with what he was doing and left for his date. Another night Sarah and Paul got stoned together. For the first time in their entire marriage Sarah approached her husband for sex. Paul rejected her advances.

"It's too late for that, Sarah. I'm getting love elsewhere now, and anyhow I don't like your smell."

She didn't answer him. She lay in bed that night recalling how terribly she and Nicholas had treated Paul. Her past conduct horrified her. She fell asleep hating herself.

***

"Is Paul driving you to the airport?"

Edith was speaking to her friend on the telephone.

"Yes, I think so."

"If he doesn't, let me know and I'll take you.

How do you feel about leaving?"

"Mixed. I believe my marriage is over, and this finalizes it."

Edith thought for a moment.

"It does seem quite hopeless."

"He's been good to me and taken all my shit. I don't blame him for wanting out. I'm surprised he waited this long. He says he'll never marry a Jewish girl again."

Edith laughed. "That was the least of his problems."

Sarah continued, ignoring Edith's remark. "Paul couldn't stand walking into the loft and finding me on the phone with you. He always felt our conversations were a waste of time, an excuse not to work."

Edith wondered if Sarah was indirectly blaming her for what was happening. She had an urge to defend herself.

"What's wrong with friends speaking with each other? I think what really bothered Paul was the knowledge I had of your affair."

"I'm sure that's true. Either way there's something very final about my going to California. I feel strangely excited, even got a pedicure, and bought a pair of shoes for $100. I also got a jumpsuit and last, but not least, I had my hair cut."

Edith was astounded. Sarah never spent money easily.

"Pedicure and jumpsuit sound just about right for Los Angeles. Don't get seduced out there. Remember to come home."

Sarah changed the subject.

"I'll miss you, Edith. Try to get some work done. I'll write to you from L.A."

Sarah was saying good-bye and Edith suspected it might be for a long time.

"Hi, I wasn't sure it was you."

Edith had seen Bill, a man she once knew, get on the bus. In the middle of debating with herself about whether or not to say hello, he saw her. Bill was a writer. Edith had gone out with him many years before. It hadn't gone too well between them. Bill had just begun to write and was insecure. Edith had been slightly contemptuous. They had never slept together because Edith didn't want to. Bill used to say, "Don't you know what's going on out there?" Edith hadn't cared what was "going on out there." She also remembered his telling her:

"You can't stand a man having problems. If a man really needed you, you wouldn't be there. You don't know how."

At the time, Edith had dismissed his remark. But as time and relationships passed, she realized a man's problems did have a way of making her uncomfortable. Bill hadn't been the only man who had spoken to her that way. When parting time came, they all said the same thing to her:

"You don't know how to share, Edith. You won't accept other people's problems. You're looking for a fantasy, Edith. It doesn't exist."

Edith remembered how tired they all made her, but wondered if they had been right.

Edith and Bill had met periodically through the years, in the street, on a bus. Edith had even called him on the phone once or twice, but he never responded. And here he was again.

"Hi, how are you?"

Bill sat down next to her and looked at his watch. It was 1:45.

"I'm going to the theater. Doesn't look like I'll make it."

Edith ignored his remark and asked a question.

"Are you still writing?"

"Yes. I returned from Hollywood to write my great American novel."

"How did you like working there?"

"After a while I didn't know if I liked the work or the money. That's when I decided to come home."

Edith secretly felt jealous. She wished it was possible for her to have his options.

"What's your great American novel about?"

"It's a court case that occurred last summer. I now spend all my time at the Tombs or in Harlem. I've got eleven months of research in my apartment. There's enough for two novels and four screenplays."

Edith was waiting for Bill to ask what she'd been doing. The question finally came.

"What have you been up to?"

"Writing."

If he was surprised, he didn't show it.

"What kind of writing?"

"Mostly short stories."

The bus was coming to her stop. Edith stood up.

"One of my stories will be published soon."

Suddenly her voice changed. It became almost pleading.

"Please call me. We could have dinner and talk. Please."

She ran off the bus before he had a chance to answer. Her face was flushed and she continued to run for no apparent reason. When she reached her apartment she searched for Bill's telephone number. Edith found it and called. Though she knew he wasn't there, her curiosity made her wonder if someone else might be. Five rings. No one answered. Edith felt satisfied. She also felt desire.

The day after meeting Bill, Edith went to a beauty salon. While she waited her turn, another memory of Bill returned. He had taken her dancing. The discotheque had been dark and romantic. Their bodies had moved very well together. They had barely spoken a word the entire evening but were well aware of one another. They had held hands quietly and the only words spoken were Bill's.

"It's nice."

This memory aroused Edith and once more she wished he would call. If not, she'd have to risk rejection and call him. The man doing her hair was flirting with her. Edith didn't respond. She was deciding what she might say to Bill if they spoke.

A week went by and Edith got no call from Bill. "I think I'll call him, invite him for dinner, ask him to read my work." With that thought, she did nothing. Edith realized she was terrified of being rejected. She spoke aloud.

"If he says no, what can I lose? At least I've tried."

Using this as a rationale, she made her way to the telephone. She called. There was no answer. Edith felt relieved, but promised herself she'd try again that evening.

Edith did try calling Bill again. This time he picked up the phone.

"Hello."

Edith took a moment to answer.

"Bill?"

"Yes."

"It's Edith. I wasn't sure if it was you or not. Your voice sounds different on the telephone."

"It's me."

"I thought you might be able to do me a favor." She didn't wait for a response, but continued. "I'd like you to read the first hundred pages of the novel I'm working on. I would like to know what you think of it."

"I'd be glad to, but I'm very busy right now."

Edith's heart sank, but she wouldn't give up.

"I don't mind waiting. It's just that I need an

opinion. You're a writer. I'd appreciate your thoughts."

"Sure. Why don't you leave it with my doorman. A friend from California sent me a manuscript so I have to read that one too. Give me ten days and I'll call you."

"Fine. Are you going to be home around 12:15? I'm usually in your neighborhood at that time."

"No. My doorman can be trusted absolutely. Just give it to him."

"Okay. Bill . . ." her voice lingered. "Never mind, I'll leave it for you."

Bill laughed.

"Speak to you soon. 'Bye."

"'Bye."

Edith hung up the telephone feeling disappointed. She'd expected to be invited for lunch or at least to his apartment. He'd done neither. She gave him every opening to see her and he paid no attention. There was nothing left to do but wait and be patient. Edith's vulnerability surprised her. She was behaving like a teenager. The more vulnerable she felt, the more she thought about John. He wouldn't have told her to "leave it with the doorman." Edith had never realized before how easily she was injured. Bill had offended her, but still she felt it important to try and reawaken those small buds of interest he had once felt for her. If it didn't happen, John was not the only alternative. She'd have to stop believing that myth and not go back to him.

The first few weeks without John had been a relief. More recently, whenever Edith felt the possibility of rejection, she felt a temptation to call him. She wanted the reassurance of being special. Her concern about her new manuscript and Bill's cool behavior frustrated her. Edith felt impotent. To manipulate John's penis would once more give her power. It was seductive, but Edith rejected the idea. She'd just begun to take chances and wouldn't allow herself to call him. Life had turned around on her or maybe she was turning around on life.

Edith's phone rang at eight o'clock in the morning.

"Hello."

She heard the underwater long distance sound and wondered who it was.

"It's Michel here."

She didn't understand. "Who?"

"Michel from Paris."

Edith sat up in bed.

"How are you Michel?"

"Very well."

"How's your work going?"

"Fine, but that's not what I called to talk about."

Edith was silent.

"Sasha had a dream about you last night."

Edith didn't know what to say. She realized Sasha must be, in Michel's words, "Miss Twenty-Five Years Old, Boy's Body, Super Brains." Edith couldn't imagine why he was telling her this, so she said nothing.

"She dreamed," Michel continued, "that you'd be returning to Paris."

"Ask her what happens to me when I get there."

"You know, Edith," Michel went on, ignoring her sarcasm, "no one can have my body any more. I'm willing to share my mind, but my body is no longer available."

"I understand, Michel," Edith answered him earnestly.

"Good. Then I'll say good-bye now."

Before Edith could say another word, he hung up. Edith got out of bed and made herself a cup of coffee. She brought the coffee back to her bed and sat wondering what that call was all about. She remembered her weeks in Paris with him, and it seemed such a long time ago. She slowly sipped her coffee and wished he hadn't called.

The phone rang again. Edith jumped and was a little afraid to answer it. "What if it's him calling back," she thought. She finally lifted the receiver as if in a trance. She felt light-headed and couldn't quite focus on anything.

"Hello."

"Hi, Edith, it's Bill."

For a moment Edith almost forgot who Bill was.

"Oh, hi." Her voice was tentative.

"I just finished reading your manuscript and thought if you had some free time now I could come over."

Edith's began to come out of her trance.

"Sure."

She suddenly felt a deep appreciation for his interest.

"I'll be there in half an hour."

Edith hung up the phone, jumped out of bed, and proceeded to wash and dress. She put on a pair of jeans and a green T-shirt that matched her eyes. She wanted to appear both sexy and casual.

Bill arrived. Edith looked at him as if seeing him for the first time. He looked nice. Nothing more, nothing less. Nice. She was struck by his lack of narcissism. His manner of dress and movement appeared spontaneous. There was nothing calculated about him. Bill placed the manuscript on her dining room table and sat down. Did he want some coffee? Some orange juice would do. Nervously Edith poured the juice. What if he didn't like her work? She was scared to death. What he said mattered.

This realization threw her into a frenzy. Half of her was above ground, the other half still submerged. If only she could extend her arms to someone to help pull her all the way out. She thought of Winnie the Pooh stuck in the rabbit hole and unable to get in or out because he had grown fat eating the rabbit's honey. She sat down and waited for Bill's judgment.

"It's good. Really good."

Edith's face flushed. Whatever he said now she could accept because he had said it was good.

"In the second half your main character must transcend herself. If you can do that, you'll have a terrific book. I found the female point of view fascinating. Look, I really liked it. You've got to finish it. If you don't, forget about your life."

Edith didn't understand why Bill was placing

the book on such life or death terms, but instinctively she knew he was right.

"When it's all finished I'll go over the whole book with you. Your syntax and grammar are awful, but after a while I liked it. Finish it. You're defining yourself. It's important for all of us to do that."

Edith remained silent. Bill finished his juice.

"I've got to go now. Let's get together next week."

"I'd like that."

This was one of the few times that Edith had said "I'd like that" to a man and meant it. She showed him to the door and kissed him lightly on the cheek.

"Thank you."

Bill ran his fingers lightly through her hair.

"Speak to you next week."

He was gone.

Edith felt happy and wished she could speak to Sarah. Instead she decided to write her a letter. No, a one line telegram would do.

"My love to you. Edith."

She lay down on her bed and thought about what Bill had said.

"If you don't finish it, forget about your life. You're defining yourself."

For the first time, she knew in her soul that there was no going back. No matter what happened she would push and squirm her way out of the rabbit hole. Bill was right. It was a matter of life and death.

Edith rang the bell to Bill's apartment. It was the first time she had ever been there and had no idea what to expect. She felt her heart beating quickly as she waited for Bill to answer the door. She heard the door being opened and swallowed hard. Her mouth had become very dry.

"Hi, come in."

Edith entered a bright, cheery apartment. A large floral print couch with a square white low coffee table in front of it were the first things that caught her eye. Books were piled on the table, barely leaving enough room for an ash tray. His large glass dining room table was trimmed with aluminum. That too was covered with books. It also had a typewriter and manuscript on it. She wondered where he ate.

"Come, I'll show you my den."

Edith followed him into another room. It looked totally organized. Book shelves covered one whole wall. A dark green corduroy couch faced the shelves. An old wooden rocking chair sat quietly in the corner.

"This is the room I like to relax and meditate in."

"It looks very conducive for that."

Edith noticed fresh flowers in both rooms. Bill must have seen her looking at them.

"Fresh flowers are the one real luxury I allow myself. I buy new ones every week."

"They're beautiful."

"Would you like to see the bedroom?"

"Sure."

Bill's bedroom was nice, but it looked like the room he cared least about. It had a large, low bed with two built-in wooden night tables, one on either side of the bed. Across from the bed was a long double dresser which looked similar to the one John owned. She didn't like being reminded of John and suddenly became uncomfortable. Edith smiled at Bill and left the room. Bill followed and they both seated themselves comfortably on the living room couch.

After a few minutes of silence, Bill stood up and left the room, returning with a bottle of red wine. Within a matter of minutes Edith felt slightly drunk.

"You're in a rage, Edith. I knew that when I read your script. I mean novel. I don't know why I keep calling it a script."

"I know I am."

They were quiet for a moment. Bill got up to put on a record. It was something by Samuel Barber. Leontyne Price sang the lyrics. Bill put the record cover in Edith's lap and told her to follow the words. Everytime she tried to speak, he told her not to.

"Don't speak. Follow the words."

Edith's head was clouded from too much wine and the beauty of the music. She kept reading, but absorbed little. Something about a child with beautiful parents living in the country and sitting on a porch. Her eyes couldn't focus because her soul felt too full. Bill removed the record cover from her lap and replaced it with a book of poetry.

"Read this poem. It's for you. The title is 'Walls'."

> With no consideration, no pity, no
> shame,
> they've built walls around me, thick and
> high.
> And now I sit here feeling hopeless.
> I can't think of anything else: this fate
> gnaws my mind
> because I had so much to do outside.
> When they were building the walls, how
> could I have not noticed?
> But I never heard the builders, not
> a sound.
> Imperceptibly they've closed me off
> from the outside world.

Edith picked up her head from the book. She looked at Bill and nodded. He seemed to know more about her than she did. The poem made her sad. Bill spoke.

"He's a great Greek poet. His name is Cafavy."

Edith asked for paper and pen. She copied the poem and placed it in her bag. Bill watched her and spoke.

"You're a sad beauty, but you've also been a selfish one. I don't think you've ever really given one thing to a man."

"Probably not. Play the Samuel Barber for me one more time and then I must go."

Bill put on the record. They sat in silence. Edith felt very emotional and wanted to leave. When the record was over, Edith stood up. Bill remained seated on the couch. Edith felt as if she might fall.

"I'm really drunk. It's hard for me to stand."

"You can sleep here if you want. I won't bother you. The couch in the den opens up into a bed if you want your privacy."

Edith felt sad that he needed to reassure her in this way. She walked to the couch and kissed the top of his head.

"You don't have to say those things. I'm not afraid of being attacked by you."

He took her hand and kissed it.

"Good night," Edith said.

"Don't you want me to take you home?"

"Not tonight."

"All right. Sleep well. I'll speak to you tomorrow."

When Edith got outside, the cool fresh air felt good on her face. She decided to walk a few blocks before hailing a taxi.

John was watching her from across the street. He had been watching her apartment for the last week and had followed her to Bill's. Now he observed her as she walked and breathed in the cool night air.

"She probably just got laid, that ungrateful bitch. I'd like to kill her."

Edith had no idea she was being spied on and enjoyed her walk. She finally stopped a cruising taxi and went home. John stared up at the bay window in her bedroom. When he saw the light go out, he left.

Edith went right to sleep. In the morning she awoke feeling strange. Bill knew who she was. No more pretending. She was both frightened and elated, wanting him to call and at the same time hoping never to speak with him again. But in the depths of her soul she knew she needed him. She placed the Cafavy poem over her bed and read it over and over. Her doorbell rang. It was the mailman. He handed her a special delivery letter. Edith knew by the handwriting who it was from. She opened it immediately, thinking something might be wrong.

Edith darling,

Since you left I have been faithful and lonely. You have no idea how much I miss you and how much I need you. I think you are the right woman for me and I mean woman in all ways. I wish I could see you. We could talk, have dinner, sleep, and make love together.

How many beautiful nights have we spent together, what a lovely time we had together. Every night when I go home I feel like screaming because you are not there. My room and my bed look so big that I feel lost—oh baby, how terrible it is. I keep thinking of all our kisses, caresses, and precious hours—lost in our paradise. We will be together again. I am sure we will because we need each other and love each other. All my love,

John

Edith was shocked. This didn't sound like John at all. For her, John had become a sad memory, but a memory just the same. She assumed he felt the same. His letter jolted her. She felt he was no longer her responsibility, but felt concerned. He had always been so cold and proud. She decided to ignore the letter, not wanting to give him any encouragement.

John's new obsession was following Edith. Every now and then he'd write her a passionate letter so she'd remember him. He'd usually feel the desire to write after seeing her with Bill. "I won't let her forget so easily," he thought. He'd sit down at his desk and write in large scrawling script, but he always addressed the envelope with his usual fine small print. He liked the special delivery touch. It gave the letter more urgency. John no longer went out with other women. Each night he stood staring at the bay window waiting to catch a glimpse of Edith. If she left her apartment, he followed her. If she remained at home, he just watched.

***

Whenever Bill and Edith weren't working, they would meet. Sometimes they met in the middle of the day and didn't part until the evening. They walked, compared ideas, and quickly became friends. For the first time in her life, Edith was sharing her deepest side with a man. Bill had known her at her worst, seemed to understand her present fears, and accepted her. She wished so much to give him something in return.

Edith didn't understand that her need for this man was very important to him. Bill knew he had to be supportive. This knowledge was giving him strength. He sensed her vulnerability and didn't want her falling backward. She had to finish that book. One evening, after returning from a walk, they sat quietly in Edith's apartment.

"Would you like a drink?"

"Sure."

Bill sat down on the living room floor while Edith prepared two vodkas. After placing the glasses on the rug, she went back for the bottle. The two of them felt relaxed. Edith stretched out on the living room rug and began to giggle. Bill bent over her to make sure she was all right. Edith's thoughts were, Do I want to kiss him? Yes, but I'm afraid.

"You know, I just realized that I'm afraid to kiss you," Edith said.

Bill smiled. "Why?"

"What if I don't know how?"

She felt like a child. Bill's voice was kind.

"Would you like to try it?"

"Yes and no."

"Well, tell me when you decide."

"I will."

Bill sat upright and sipped his drink. He looked at Edith and spoke.

"The apartment seems very quiet, doesn't it?"

"I think I'd like you to kiss me now."

Bill put down his drink and lay next to her. Edith turned her head to look at him. He gently stroked her hair and moved his head close to hers. He brushed her lips tenderly with his own. Edith continued to watch him. He took her finger and placed it to his lips. She took his finger away and kissed it. Bill smiled at her, and suddenly they were kissing with passion. Edith couldn't stop. Their tongues met inside each other's mouth. They licked one another's faces and then returned to their lips. Finally it was over. Edith never remembered kissing anyone like that before. She didn't know it was possible to derive so much pleasure and sensuality from a kiss. Bill lay staring at the ceiling.

"I'd say, for someone who didn't think she could kiss, you did pretty good."

"God, I could have gone on all night."

"Some night we will, but not tonight. Believe it or not, I have to meet a man in Harlem in a little while."

Edith understood. For the first time she really understood. Bill helped her up from the floor. They walked arm in arm to the door. Edith caught her reflection in the mirror. Her hair was tousled and her face wiped clean of makeup.

"You're seeing the real me."

She touched her hair self-consciously.

"You look great," Bill said, and kissed her gently on the lips. "I'll speak to you tomorrow."

He left. The apartment was silent, but if someone listened very hard, the sound of a woman singing could be heard.

***

John watched Bill as he left the apartment building and got into a cab. "I wonder what that whore was doing up there," he thought. He began kicking the ground. A pebble bounced a few inches in front of him. John picked it up, looked at it, and hurled it in the direction of Edith's large bay window. It fell short of its mark, but John was satisfied.

"That's for being a bad, bad girl."

Since Bill had left, John felt no great need to continue his vigil. "She's not going out anymore," he said aloud. Passersby were looking at him, but John didn't notice. As he began to walk, he suddenly felt panicked and broke out in a sweat. He then began to run.

"Look at me, everyone. I'm a gazelle. I'm a gazelle."

Edith lay in bed that night and thought about Bill. She felt anxious. Her shyness overwhelmed her and she realized she was terrified of sleeping with him. All those years of pornographic sex had left her unprepared for real feelings. To kiss was one thing. Total exposure was something else. She wondered if she had really made love ever in her entire life. She knew Bill would be patient and give her time, but she still couldn't shake the anxiety. What if she failed? Maybe she was a lousy lover. Her naked body might even repulse him. John, or any of the other Johns in her life, had satisfied her. But that game didn't work any more. She was left with who she really was, a shy, frightened woman. This was not the case with her work. There she was bold and daring, loving to shock—a rebel to the world, an insecure child to herself. If only she knew how to merge her two selves, integrate, be whole. Something still held her back and that something was sex. She wanted to talk with someone, reveal herself, hear a reaction. Edith decided to call Sarah in California. She needed her friend's help. She dialed direct to the Zen Center and waited for Sarah to come to the phone.

"Edith, I'm so glad to hear from you."

"How are you, Sarah?"

"Well, if nothing else, I'm learning a little discipline."

"What are you doing there?"

"Believe it or not, I get up at four in the morning, then I do my sitting and working until eleven at night. It's really hard for me. I don't know how much longer I can take this kind of Japanese torture, but I'd like to stick it out as long as possible. What's happening with you?"

Edith explained her situation with Bill.

"I really felt like I didn't know how to kiss. Everytime we're alone together I get nervous. Sometimes I even think about sleeping with John again and telling Bill. It's almost as if I want him to hate me. Then I'd be free of this damned anxiety. Occasionally I wonder how I'd feel if he found someone else and wasn't there for me. I'm also afraid he'll die. These thoughts panic me. I've come to depend on his support. I'd feel lost without him, but I'm in real terror over the sex."

Sarah finally spoke.

"Maybe you're just not attracted to him."

"I wish it were that simple. I've slept with far less attractive men, only I hated them. If it was just that, I wouldn't have all this anxiety. Kissing him was lovely. I felt warm and good. When he left, I felt relaxed, sang, felt content. After sex with other men I'd usually make a phone call and forget the whole experience. This time I savored it and wanted nothing from the outside world to intrude."

"It sounds like you're in love."

"Maybe I am. God, maybe I really am."

"It's about time one of us did something right. Stick with it. I'll call you next week. Maybe you'll have slept with him by then."

"Take care, Sarah. My love to you. 'Bye."

The phone clicked dead. Edith put down the receiver. "If Bill and I ever do make love, I'll never discuss it with anyone," she thought.

***

Bill and Edith made a tentative date for dinner. When she called Bill to confirm their plans, his voice sounded cold.

"We're off tomorrow night. One of my scripts got turned down today."

"Do you know why?"

"No!" His voice was angry. "It doesn't fit any genre. Well, I'm not a genre, I'm me."

Edith spoke gently. "The only thing any of us can do is keep going and support one another."

"It's not good enough, Edith."

He didn't give her a chance to say one more word.

"I'll speak to you over the weekend. Maybe we can get together."

He hung up. Edith felt terrible. She didn't know how to bury her hurt and disappointment. She began to blame herself. Maybe Bill thought she didn't want to be alone with him. Maybe, maybe, maybe. She tried rationalizing the pain away. "Who needs him? I have my writing. I'm getting a story published." The pain remained. She felt as if she was involved in the most torrid love affair, feeling so vulnerable.

The weather had suddenly turned hot. Edith felt suffocated in her apartment. Her head started to pound. Her eyes felt heavy. It was too hot to work. She took two aspirin. She lay down on her bed and began to read. Within minutes she was asleep.

She woke to the sound of something being

shoved under her door. Edith felt slightly dazed when she went to investigate the noise. An envelope lay on the floor. She picked it up, still feeling drowsy. She was aware of having a terrible taste in her mouth.

"I think I'll brush my teeth."

She placed the unopened envelope on the toilet seat while she freshened herself. When she felt better, her curiosity took over. She quickly opened the letter.

> I'M WATCHING YOU ALL THE TIME. ARE YOU HAVING FUN WITH YOUR NEW BOYFRIEND? I'VE TURNED INTO A GAZELLE. I FEEL LIKE KILLING YOU BUT PROBABLY WILL RESTRAIN MYSELF
>
> BUT
>
> DON'T COUNT ON IT. I LIKE FOLLOWING YOU. YOU HAVE A NICE ASS.
>
> GUESS WHO.

Edith tossed the note into the garbage as if it were contaminated. Who would play such a horrible prank, she wondered. Her hands were shaking. "Maybe it was placed under the wrong door." She sat down on her bed and sighed.

"It's John. Of course, it's John."

Edith left her apartment with a purpose. She

wanted to see if John was anywhere in sight. She remembered that John still had the keys to her apartment. I'll get the locks changed immediately, she thought. As she made her way to the locksmith, she turned around often to see if John was behind her. He was nowhere to be seen.

"We can't change the locks for you today, lady."

"Why not? It's important."

"Look, if I could I would. You think I don't want the business?"

"Well then, what's the problem?"

"I'm here by myself. My men are all out. You can look for yourself."

"That's all right. When can you send someone to my apartment?"

"Not before tomorrow afternoon."

"All right. I'll expect you then."

"Not me, lady, one of my men. I never leave the shop."

Edith gave him a dirty look and wrote down her name and address.

"He'd never hurt me," mumbled Edith to herself. All the same, she dreaded returning to her apartment.

The next day the anxiety was gone. The locks were changed and Edith laughed at her fear of the day before. She had a fleeting thought of John and then decided it was probably some nut who was putting notes under everyone's door. John might be a degenerate, but she didn't think he was dangerous. She looked at herself in the bathroom mirror.

"I look pretty today," she thought. "It's too bad Bill won't see me. Who needs him and all that anxiety anyway? Forget it, Edith, and get back to work."

That evening she thought about calling him. For the first time it entered her head that he might be with another woman. Maybe someone he slept with. No, she wouldn't call him. Too risky. Was he spiting her? Was he sick of her shyness and fear. Edith believed she would never hear from Bill again. She couldn't get beyond her own needs. It finally occurred to her as she prepared for bed that Bill's script had been rejected. She, however, had thought of nothing but her own hurt feelings. She vowed to call him over the weekend and bury her false pride.

The weekend went by without Edith and Bill speaking. Neither one had called the other. Every time Edith approached the phone she thought of his last words to her.

"I'll speak to you over the weekend. Maybe we can get together."

She felt angry. "He said he'd call. I'll be damned if I call him." Yet he was a friend, so why should Edith stand on ceremony? It never mattered who called whom. "He promised, and I won't call him first," she thought.

So Edith spent the weekend without him and

went to two old Marlene Dietrich movies: *Shanghai Express* and *Betrayed.* They made her wonder if communication between the sexes could ever exist. If the beautiful Dietrich had such problems, what chance did she have?

She received no more notes and dismissed the incident. By the time Monday rolled around, Edith felt better. The sun was shining and a new week beginning. She immediately went to work on her manuscript. FUCK HIM she wrote on a fresh sheet of typewriter paper. Her week had begun.

Bill hadn't called Edith because he felt disappointed in himself. He wondered about his ability to help her.

Bill was no exception to the fear of rejection. All the work that mattered to him never got into print; only his California television writing earned him a living and that he hated. He felt discouraged and didn't want it to rub off on Edith. Instead of calling her as he'd promised, he went to the country for the weekend. A friend owned a house in Bridgehampton and Bill welcomed the idea of getting away from the city for two days.

When he thought about Edith, his feelings were mixed. Her extreme vulnerability concerning sex unnerved him. He understood she would have to come to him sexually. Maybe that's why he'd disappeared for the weekend without telling her. It was a combination of spite and frustration, but also a feeling that it was important for her to know he wasn't there for the asking. She'd have to come to accept and value him as he did her. If it was cowardly to run away for the weekend without an explanation, she'd have to understand it. Otherwise their friendship was worth little. Bill wanted Edith, but only on terms that were acceptable to both of them.

Bill knew she was used to being adored but not loved. Bill didn't adore her. He recognized her selfishness and narcissism, but also felt he knew her soul and knew they were mates. To be firm and loving at the same time was difficult. He thought about calling her from the country but decided against it. Sometimes it was important to disappear and for Bill this was one of those times. He took long walks and thought about Edith's confession of fear over a kiss. It made him smile. He felt protective and didn't want to hurt her. He knew real friends couldn't hurt one another and hoped to push through her layers of fear to become her friend. Only then could they be lovers. Bill was a patient man.

After receiving Edith's phone call, Sarah decided to write her a letter. It was difficult. Her head spun with thoughts about the Zen Center and her work with roshi. She could feel Edith's condemnation even thousands of miles away. She also knew Edith wouldn't say anything but in her silence there was a fierce judgment. Sarah didn't know if she had come to the Center looking for an escape from her life, or if she had found a new enforced discipline which she thought she needed. This particular Zen Center had a few Hollywood stars staying there. If they could serve roshi totally, by waiting on him and doing menial tasks, certainly Sarah could give it a try. She decided to sit at the Zen Center for two weeks. She had told Edith the truth about having to get up at four A.M. and sitting and working until eleven P.M. It was hard for her and she meant it when she referred to this kind of schedule as a kind of Japanese torture, but she wanted to try and work it out.

It was a relief to know that Harold Berg, a waning, whining folk singer she once knew, was also there. He was a pal and an old pal at that. Sarah had once had him on her list of magic men and was surprised to find herself completely relaxed with him. She felt her relationship with Nicholas had made a permanent change in the way she now related to the men she'd once been afraid of. Harold, whose marriage had been full of passion and nightmares, said "Marriage was the cemetery. It's the place where you can rest."

Sarah certainly knew what he meant, and he was very funny—especially when he discussed his escapades with women. Everyone at the Zen Center seemed to appreciate the difficulties of working out a marriage—even roshi, who had recently married.

Sarah tried to concentrate on the letter she was supposed to be writing. But as she looked at the empty sheet of paper, her head continued to reel with her own thoughts.

I don't know what I'm doing . . . not in my realm to decide . . . unable to think in terms of my split with Paul . . . just can't . . . maybe sitting will relieve or change something . . . as if anyone was there holding their breath.

Paul had called her that morning. He said Lincoln Center was possibly interested in his film for the festival. It had passed one round of judges, so it had a fifty-fifty chance. Sarah told him she thought it was great news. He then went on to tell her of his difficulties in getting started with another idea. She told him she'd be in California for at least three weeks.

"Long time," Paul said.

They hung up on each other with nothing resolved. Only the sadness remained. Her mind continued to wander.

"If I go from minute to minute there should be no fear of the future. Fear is really a foolish obstacle and I'm tired of it."

Maybe her thoughts were too glib about the Zen Center. She felt roshi to be one of the most evolved men in the country . . . truly. Sarah sometimes thought he possibly was even already dead and just doing a practice here on earth. She looked down at her writing paper and wondered how Edith was doing. She'd write tomorrow. She hoped her friend was involved with a decent man and doing lots of good work. Yes, she'd write tomorrow. It was time for her to brush up on her letter writing. She hadn't done it for a while. As a matter of fact she hadn't thought in a while. It really felt good to take a fly with some thought. That's why it was important to sit at the Center . . . to get into it and open up a little space in her head.

She'd write tomorrow and send her love to everyone. Today she felt too tired. She'd been trying to switch her sleeping habits over to five hours a night instead of almost nine. By mid-afternoon she was ready to call it quits. Sarah's head drooped and in a moment's time she was asleep.

In spite of the Japanese torture, Sarah felt good at the Zen Center. The people there became her family and roshi was the big daddy of them all. Sarah admired him most for his ordinary ways. He took tea with his disciples and would always eat one cake too many, which explained his bulging stomach. He complained about his marriage like everyone else and was fond of saying that "life was a preparation for death, and death was a preparation for life." This made Sarah think of herself as always evolving. If only she could really believe it. For most of her adult life she had felt stuck in unrelenting pain. Pain in her eyes, her bones, everywhere.

Roshi's words comforted her and she began to think of her film. Here she was in sunny California, surrounded by the myths that had formed her life. She was struck with an idea. She decided to take slides from the old movies she loved most and insert them in her own film: *Duel in the Sun, To Have and Have Not,* lots of Robert Mitchum movies. He had always been a favorite. She was pleased with the idea; it felt clean, almost like an industrial film. Sarah had friends who could gain access to the studios for her. It would mean staying in California for longer than she had planned, but she decided to do it.

Within a week's time she was ready to shoot the footage. The sequence was shot in one day. Sarah couldn't believe it. The first part of her film, which ran only fifteen minutes, had taken her almost three years to complete. This second part was ten minutes long and it only took her a week. This alone made her trip worth while. She sent the footage to the lab. When it was finished she looked at it through an editing machine. It was good. She felt it added to her film because it destroyed some of the myths of her past. What a relief. Now, when she returned to New York, it would be with a sense of accomplishment.

***

Bill finally did call Edith. His disappearance was not mentioned. Edith was so pleased to hear his voice that she forgot she was ever angry.

"When do you want to have dinner?" The words came tumbling out of her mouth as if she had no control over them.

"Well, I'm pretty busy this week but let's try for Friday."

This was only Tuesday. Edith wanted it more definite.

"I'll have some new pages for you to read by Friday."

"Good. I'll call you during the day. If we can't make it Friday, then definitely over the weekend," Bill said.

"Okay, I'll speak to you Friday, 'Bye, love."

Why did she call him love? Edith hated that expression. Did her anxiety also cause her to use insincere phrases? Still, his call had made her happy. She wished he had been a little more definite but felt confident she'd see him that Friday. Edith thought about their conversation. She couldn't accept the fact that it had been imperfect. There had been moments of awkwardness when they had both spoken at the same time.

"Big deal, so we spoke at the same time."

Even Edith was becoming bored with her fears. She returned to her typewriter, but something distracted her. It was the familiar sound of an envelope being slipped under her door.

"Not again," she thought. This time she hoped to catch the lunatic off guard. She opened the door, but saw no one. The hall was deserted. Suddenly she felt afraid and quickly closed the door. She made sure to turn the double lock.

> EDITH DEAR
> AREN'T YOU GETTING TIRED OF STAYING AT HOME ALONE WEEK-ENDS? DOESN'T YOUR NEW BOY-FRIEND LIKE TO BE WITH YOU? IT MUST SUCK IN BED. SPEAKING OF SUCK, I'D LOVE YOU TO SUCK ME.

DO YOU KNOW WHO ME IS? YOU SHOULD.
I'M WATCHING YOU, SO BE CAREFUL.

Edith had thrown out the other note, but decided to keep this one. She was beginning to feel frightened and wanted to show the note to Bill.

***

John liked tormenting Edith. He even enjoyed the feeling of losing control of himself. He had bought himself a gun. Sometimes he'd stand naked in front of his long mirror and point the gun at his reflection. He liked to pretend he was a gangster, and perfected his Humphrey Bogart and James Cagney imitations for the benefit of his image in the looking glass.

"Okay gang, you're going to do what I say and like it."

He'd keel over in laughter and go on to another pose. John Wayne usually came next.

"Draw your gun. For God's sake, draw!"

He didn't like this role as much and usually returned to being Humphrey Bogart.

Sometimes while following Edith or staring at her bay window, he'd think he was Sam Spade, private detective, doing a job for a client. He'd take notes on where Edith went and who she spoke to. "She talked to a tall, blond lady walking a poodle." He liked to read them over at night and file them away.

During the day, however, John remained the upright business man, wheeling and dealing. Above all, he continued to maintain the respect of the business community. At least three charities wanted him as a guest speaker for their causes. He turned them all down. His nights were his own and he liked keeping watch over Edith.

***

Bill called Edith on Friday afternoon, as he had promised.

"I have a surprise for you."

Edith became excited. She loved surprises.

"I took a suite for us at the Sherry Netherlands. You once mentioned that you loved hotel rooms, so I decided to splurge and feel good."

Edith was shocked. This was the last thing she'd expected from unpretentious Bill. She fell silent. Her thoughts were running quickly. What did he expect them to do in this elegant suite of his?

"Don't worry, Edith. No pressure. We can have room service and watch television all night if you want."

"In other words, we're going to pretend to be in

another country."

"Something like that. It's just a way of being extravagant, of feeling good. These last two weeks have been rotten."

Edith suddenly felt amused.

"How do we work this? Do I meet you in the hotel room, or present myself with you at the front desk?"

"Whichever way you're most comfortable. I already have the room so you can just meet me there, if you'd prefer."

"Okay. Let's say seven-thirty. What's the room number?"

"1713."

"See you later."

Edith hung up the receiver and wondered what Bill really had in mind. She began to feel uncomfortable. A strange realization struck her: she didn't want to see him naked. Was it her nakedness, or his nakedness that frightened her? She didn't think it was the female body that bothered her. Bill's maleness made her angry. She pictured his penis being small.

Edith wondered what it was in her that produced such repugnance toward the male body, especially toward a man she admired and respected. Why think about the size of his penis, his chest, the whiteness of his skin? She couldn't answer her questions, but wondered just the same.

However mixed her feelings were about being with Bill in bed, she certainly felt no conflict about going to a hotel. It seemed both romantic and illicit, and Edith loved room service.

She dressed with great care that evening. A pair of bikini underpants was the first item placed on her body. She then put on a white peasant blouse. The strings that held the blouse firmly closed were left open. She draped a coral necklace around her neck. It had been a gift given to her mother. Her mother's idea of jewelry was pearls, not coral beads so she had given them to Edith. Black slacks and black patent leather high-heeled sandals completed her outfit. She was pleased with the way she looked and left her apartment feeling good.

Edith arrived at the Sherry Netherlands right on time.

John watched her from across the street and wondered what she was doing there.

Edith had remembered to take that horrible note with her to show Bill. She walked with great confidence directly to the elevator but she was sure that all eyes were upon her as she made her way through the lobby. When she gave the floor number to the elevator man, Edith thought he looked at her in a funny way. "He must think I'm meeting a married man," she thought.

Bill opened the door for her and they hugged for a moment. He was wearing dungarees and a plaid sport shirt. He certainly didn't look the part of a cheating husband. Edith pushed her body away from his and began to explore her surroundings. There was a grand view of Manhattan and Central Park. Edith looked at Bill and spoke.

"Do you indulge in this type of thing often?"

"No, only when I want to give myself a treat. I'm glad you're here with me to enjoy it. We can get drunk, stoned, eat, sleep, whatever we feel like doing."

Edith sat down on one of the chairs and removed her shoes.

"Let's start with dinner. I'm hungry."

Room service arrived. Bill insisted on serving Edith in bed. She thought it was a lovely idea. Her slacks came off but her blouse remained on. She slipped under the sheet while Bill placed her dinner on a tray before her. He then put on the television.

"This is paradise," said Edith, and Bill looked happy.

"I'm glad you're pleased."

They ate in silence. Both were absorbed in the movie on the television. It was an old Humphrey Bogart movie, *The Maltese Falcon*. When they had finished eating, Bill took a joint from his jacket pocket. Within seconds Edith was high. She felt good and gradually her inhibitions began fading. Bill looked at her.

"Why don't you take that blouse off?"

Suddenly it seemed like a good idea. Edith slipped it over her head. Bill watched her.

"You have beautiful breasts."

"Thank you."

Bill proceeded to undress. His body looked lean and firm. They began to kiss. Edith didn't remember the television being turned off but was aware that it was no longer on. The two of them were high and happy in this strange hotel room only a few blocks away from Edith's apartment. After they kissed and touched for a while, Bill asked Edith if she wanted her dessert. Edith was both surprised and slightly confused by his question.

"Doesn't he want me?" she wondered. Bill got out of bed and brought Edith her chocolate cake and coffee. He did the same for himself. The television remained off.

"Nice to be here, isn't it?"

Edith feigned indifference when she answered him.

"Uh-huh."

Bill looked at her. "What's wrong?"

"I guess I feel unloved."

Bill smiled and put down his plate.

"You mean because I didn't make love to you right away?"

Edith was embarrassed and felt childish. She didn't answer.

"We have all night. I have no intention of letting you out of here without making love to you. If you wanted it, you should have told me."

Edith continued picking at her dessert with her fork. Bill bent over and kissed her.

"Sometimes you're a real baby."

Edith looked up at him and spoke quietly. "I know. Part of me is three years old and the other part is three hundred years old."

"From the look of your body, I'd put you anywhere between twenty and thirty."

Edith smiled, enjoying the compliment. Bill got

out of bed.

"Let's explore the other rooms."

Edith followed. She didn't know if it was the effect of the grass, but she felt totally uninhibited about her naked body. They walked into the living room, turned out the lights, and looked at the view. In each room the view was different. It reminded her of Paris and being in Michel's apartment. That seemed so distant, almost as if it had never really happened at all. Edith was sad that it became so difficult to keep memories alive. Yet they did have a way of coming back. The view had brought Michel back to her, but only for a moment. Edith suddenly felt a chill.

"I'm cold. Let's go back to bed."

"You go. I'll be right there."

Edith returned to bed and once more got under the sheets. She couldn't help feeling slightly insulted by Bill's cool. It never occurred to her that he might be nervous. She felt stupid just lying in bed waiting. She put the television back on and watched. She really wasn't hearing or seeing anything, but she pretended she was. Bill returned to the bed.

"Anything good on?"

Edith shrugged. Bill turned the television off and placed his naked body very close to Edith's. They explored each other's faces. Bill looked different close up. Edith pushed her head back a little to see him from further away. He looked more familiar to her at a distance.

"What are you doing?"

"Looking at you from different angles."

"You trying to see which way you like me the best?"

"Not necessarily. It interests me that your face changes."

"So does yours."

Edith returned to Bill's arms and they remained like that for a while. A drowsiness swept over her and she almost fell asleep. Bill's hand slowly began to caress her. He moved his hand over her entire body, trying to get to know it. His hand felt good to Edith, very gentle and not threatening in any way. She became aroused and any fears she might have once had disappeared. Bill's hands were reassuring. She could tell by his touch that he liked the shape and feel of her body. This gave her confidence. She had never made love without sharing sexual fantasies. That was what had always excited her the most. This time it was just she and Bill, with no fantasies to arouse her. Edith felt Bill's erection under the sheets. She felt shy about touching it. Bill must have read her thoughts. He took Edith's hand and placed it on his penis.

"That's for you, Edith. Tell me when you want it."

He was giving her control, which made her shy. When she had to fight for control, she demanded. Now that all she had to do was ask, she wasn't sure she knew how.

They kissed, caressed, and all the while Edith's hand remained motionless. She began to feel unsexy, foolish, afraid to speak. She was becoming confused. She felt like an old-fashioned boy who only fucked the whore, but never the girl he loved. Bill helped her.

"Would you like me inside you?"

"Yes."

Bill got on top of Edith and without any trouble entered her. Edith, who always kept her eyes open and the lights on when she made love, closed her eyes. His motion inside her helped her to relax. She felt her vagina become wetter.

"You feel good, Edith."

The sound of his voice surprised her and she opened her eyes. Bill smiled at her. She smiled back and the fun began. Bill moved her body in various positions. They adjusted themselves and laughed at their awkward moments. For the first time in her life, Edith realized sex was supposed to be fun. She and Bill were playful.

"Let's try that mirror over there."

Edith thought that was a wonderful idea. They watched themselves for a while and then returned to the bed. Bill pulled out of her and lit a cigarette for each of them. After finishing their cigarettes, they greedily returned to each other's bodies.

It was finally over. Bill had satisfied her. She had held nothing back. Bill was equally content. Edith turned her back to him. He put his arms warmly around her. They said nothing and soon both were sleeping. His penis had been just the right size.

John sat on a park bench waiting for Edith to leave the hotel. After a few hours of sitting, he looked at his watch. It was eleven o'clock. "Where the hell was she?" he wondered. John felt hungry and tired. He bought himself two hot dogs from a vendor and devoured them. He returned to his bench and waited. He watched the people go by. Their faces looked distorted. Their noses were too long, their lips were too thick. He had trouble finding their eyes. They seemed lost in the big moon faces he thought he saw.

"How ugly people are," he thought. One middle-aged woman walked by him and he spat at her.

"You're a real witch lady, a real witch. Did you forget to bring your broomstick with you to-night?"

The woman looked at him and quickened her pace. He stood up from the bench and continued to scream after her.

"Witches like you should be locked up. There should be a jail for witches, a witch prison. You'd have plenty of company, you fat cow."

She was already out of earshot but John seemed unconcerned. He sat down again and began to laugh. He laughed so hard that tears came to his eyes. He lay down on the bench in a state of exhaustion.

"God, that witch looked familiar," he thought. Soon he was asleep.

He awoke the next morning and didn't know where he was. Then he remembered.

"Damn it! I'll never know what Edith was doing in that hotel."

People were staring at him. He looked like such

a well-dressed bum. John hailed a taxi and returned to his apartment. He overpaid the driver and mumbled something to the doorman. As he entered his apartment to ready himself for work, he wondered why everyone looked so familiar to him. His gun was casually resting on his night table as if it were nothing more than an ash tray. John thought about taking it to work with him, but instead put it in a drawer.

"Work is no place for guns."

John ate breakfast. He was starved. In a matter of minutes he devoured two fried eggs, a glass of juice, a glass of milk, five slices of toast with jam, and two large cups of coffee. He still felt starved, but he also felt sick. He went to the bathroom and vomited up everything he had just eaten. He then showered, shaved, put on his best pin-striped suit, and left for work.

"I'll have my breakfast at the office."

His stomach felt so empty that he couldn't wait to get there.

—

Edith and Bill were eating breakfast in their hotel room. Edith had just told Bill about the two notes she had received under her door.

"Do you have them with you?"

"The first one I threw away, but I brought the latest one with me."

"Let me see it."

Edith took the note out of her bag and handed it to Bill. He read it out loud.

EDITH DEAR
AREN'T YOU GETTING TIRED OF STAYING AT HOME ALONE WEEK-ENDS? DOESN'T YOUR NEW BOY-FRIEND LIKE TO BE WITH YOU? IT MUST SUCK IN BED. SPEAKING OF SUCK, I'D LOVE YOU TO SUCK ME. DO YOU KNOW WHO ME IS? YOU SHOULD.
I'M WATCHING YOU, SO BE CARE-FUL.

"God, it sounds even creepier to hear it out loud."

"Edith, this is no joke. You're obviously being watched by someone who sounds crazy. Do you have any idea who it might be?"

"I know it seems like a horrible thing to say, but I suspected John."

Bill looked at her quizzically. Edith had told him a little of her relationship with John, but she had omitted telling him about his pornographic phone calls to Sarah.

"Don't you think that's being a bit extreme? Lots of couples break up. Did he ever do anything that would make you think he was capable of this kind of craziness?"

Edith sat very still and bit on her cuticles. She haltingly told Bill about John's lewd calls to Sarah. Bill listened. When she was finished speaking, he reached his hand across the table and covered Edith's hand with his own.

"I'm sorry you've hated yourself so much."

Tears welled in Edith's eyes. She was deeply moved by Bill's understanding. He continued to speak, his voice calm.

"I think you should show this to the police."

"They wouldn't do anything based on this."

Edith had watched enough police shows on television to know that.

"Probably not, but I think you'd lose nothing by speaking to them. I'll go with you if you want."

"No, I think I'll wait a bit. I'm not sure it's John. Maybe whoever it is will go away."

"Nothing just goes away, Edith."

"Maybe this will. I sure hope so. It's starting to get on my nerves."

"I'll stay with you if you want me to."

Edith was caught off guard. She smiled but didn't say anything.

"Why don't you think about it," said Bill.

"Okay, I will."

***

Sarah finally returned from California. The first thing she did was show Paul the new segment of her film.

"I don't like it. It doesn't make sense to me. I don't know what you're trying to say by showing slides from old movies, and I don't see the connection to part one."

"I can't explain what I'm trying to do, it just feels right," answered Sarah.

"I don't see how placing a slide of *Duel in the Sun* on a board tells your audience anything."

It's strange that he picked on that particular slide, thought Sarah. That was the movie which reminded her most of herself and Nicholas. The last scene with Gregory Peck and Jennifer Jones moving toward each other and shooting guns at one another was something she pictured could have happened between her and her lover. The feelings of love and hate were so close, it was hard to tell the two emotions apart. Sarah was sorry that Paul didn't like her work, and decided to show it to Edith.

The two women sat in an editing room looking at the film.

"I love it," said Edith enthusiastically.

"All those fucking Hollywood myths that we really believed," she continued, "and based our lives on. I remember being nine years old and seeing *The Dolly Sisters* with Betty Grable and June Haver. They sang "On the Boardwalk in Atlantic City," and I thought they were the most beautiful women I'd ever seen. One day my parents told me we were going to Atlantic City for the weekend. I couldn't sleep all week picturing the beautiful people I was going to see dancing and singing."

Edith looked up at Sarah and asked,

"Have you ever been to Atlantic City?"

Sarah shook her head.

"It's dismal. The boardwalk is filled with old people sitting in wheelchairs with blankets wrapped around their legs. I couldn't believe it and cried the entire time."

"I'm glad you like what I did," said Sarah. "I was a little upset when Paul didn't get it."

Suddenly Sarah began to moan. "Oh God, there's a monstrous water bug on the floor."

Edith took one look and was instantly revolted. She began making her way to the door.

"I'm a total coward where bugs are concerned, especially ones that size. I'll wait outside the door while you kill it."

Sarah looked at her friend and knew she meant it. Edith made her way into the hall outside the editing room, and listened as Sarah bravely killed the bug. Sarah's voice could be clearly heard as she spoke to Edith in the hall.

"Edith, you're disgusting standing out there and leaving me to kill this thing alone. Oh God, oh God, this is horrible."

Edith felt guilty but didn't move. Finally Sarah opened the door. They both sat down, exhausted. Sarah spoke first.

"I just can't stand killing anything anymore. I can't even pick a flower or pull a blade of grass."

"Where did you put the bug?"

"It's in the corner underneath a piece of paper."

"Let's get out of here and take a walk."

Sarah nodded and took her film off the editing machine. The two friends left the room as fast as possible. The dead bug remained hidden in the corner.

They walked slowly up Sixth Avenue.

"I liked being at the Zen Center. It makes me feel

secure just knowing it's there."

"Do you think you'll go back?"

"I don't know. Now that I'm home, everything is the same. Paul and I still don't have sex. He hasn't resolved his love affair, though I don't think it's very important. We like each other and hug and kiss, but generally we put one another to sleep."

"You know, Sarah, he's not going to leave. For once in your life, if you want to separate, you're the one who's going to have to move and initiate the action. He's got nothing to lose by staying. You're much more vulnerable. Paul can justifiably go out with other women. He doesn't want a child, and you're forty. He's only thirty-one."

"I know all that. You can also add that there's no work around right now, and I feel my days are aimless. It throws me back to a bad spot. Nicholas pops into my head and then the old longings return. Sometimes a convent is the only place I want to be."

"Or the Zen Center."

"Or the Zen Center," repeated Sarah in very quiet tones.

Paul had promised Sarah to shoot the last segment of her film. She wanted to be in it, so obviously someone else had to work the camera. He hated the film and wished she had gotten someone else. Her slow pace and indefinite ideas drove him crazy. He wished she had more of the

Protestant work ethic in her instead of her acting the soulful Jew. By the time the day was over and the ten minute sequence was shot, Paul felt ready to kill her. It wasn't her artiness that so tore at his nerves. It was the fogginess of her thoughts that really bothered him.

He was determined to make her leave him, and had decided to try not to return to their old friendliness. He realized that that would only prolong their situation, stretching out the inevitable. His affair wasn't going very well. Paul admired his lady friend's spirit and mind, but not her body. It made him wonder about his own fear of sex, and if mutual fear was what kept his marriage going. He'd find out soon. No more kissing and cooing, no more baby talk to make them laugh together. He was determined to have one of them leave and he preferred that Sarah be the one.

Sarah knew at dinner that Paul wanted out. He was so cold and removed, just speaking long enough to criticize her. She thought about the dead water bug in the editing room and how she'd killed it. Her marriage was also dead and she felt she had killed that too. Sarah realized she'd failed to see Paul's finesse and appreciate his patience and good spirits. Now it was too late and time to go. But where to and to whom? If she worked this out, maybe she'd finally be free.

***

Edith was finally in love and she was stuck with it. She could neither control her own emotions nor Bill's. That fact made her anxious. She wondered if she could hang on to those feelings and not run away. Her first instinct was never to see Bill again, but she wanted him. As Edith sat at her typewriter staring into space, she realized she had always run away from what she'd wanted.

"This time, I'm putting myself on the line. Bill has wiped the slate clean for me. No more John, or men like him. Bill is real."

She realized she was talking out loud and felt embarrassed by the sound of her own voice. "I'm really getting peculiar," she thought. She wanted reassurance and wished Bill would talk more of her beauty, talent, intelligence. Bill was good to her but he didn't treat her as special. Edith noticed he was equally nice to everyone and extremely well liked by both sexes. Women were always calling him, sometimes just to chat or ask him for advice. At first the calls made Edith jealous, but now she was used to it. In some strange way, she even felt that she and Bill were married.

Edith continued to stare into space and think about the night they had had dinner together and Bill had forgotten to bring his glasses. He'd been unable to read the menu. Edith had read it aloud to him. There'd been a sexiness to it, a sensuality that goes along with being with your real mate. That small act had made her feel like his wife. The problem was that Edith had no idea what he was feeling. Slowly she'd made discoveries about his past. A mutual friend had told Edith that Bill's father had been a famous writer. Bill had changed his last name to avoid comparison. She remembered questioning him about his father.

"Was it difficult to be his son?"

"Yes, very difficult."

"What kind of father was he?"

"Cold, demanding. Everything I did wasn't good enough. When he did speak to me, it was usually to give me criticism. Now that he's dead I wonder if I should continue to fight for his ideas or let them go. He was a man way ahead of his time."

"What about your mother?"

"She was great. Generous, warm, only she died when I was twenty. Even at that age, I missed her."

Edith felt Bill was his father's son, no matter how hard he tried to fight it. She had read his father's books and knew what giant steps Bill would have to follow in. He'd have to risk being vulnerable and failing. Edith wanted to help him. For the first time she wanted to assist a man, and she hoped he could accept it. Edith stopped musing and snapped her mind back to her work. She looked down at the blank piece of paper in her typewriter and realized she was wasting the day. She quickly picked up her work from the day before and read it over. She began to type. Every moment was becoming precious to her.

Edith arrived at Bill's apartment for dinner. Much to her surprise she found a woman sitting there. Bill introduced them.

"Edith Dorlen, Liz Weston. Liz is doing a book on my father and needed some information from me."

Liz looked at Edith.

"I'm just about finished."

She continued to remain seated. Edith poured herself a glass of wine and wondered if Liz ever really planned to leave. Bill was being his usual polite charming self. There was finally a silence. Liz again looked at Edith.

"Where do you have your hair done? It's fantastic."

Edith couldn't believe her ears. What did her hair have to do with Bill's father?

"I do it myself, nothing to it."

Edith was lying. She had no intention of telling this woman anything, not even the name of her hairdresser. Bill must have read Edith's thoughts, for he stood up.

"If I can be of any help to you in the future, let me know."

The interview was over and Liz Weston was being ushered to the door. Bill returned to Edith and put his arm around her.

"She's written some really good articles on my father."

Edith looked at him slyly.

"I'm sure she'll want to do one on you next. Probably in bed."

"Probably, but she's too ugly."

Edith laughed and kissed him. Once more she had the feeling of being his wife. She wondered if he'd ever marry. They left the apartment to have dinner in their favorite restaurant. This time Bill remembered his glasses. There was no need for Edith to read the menu to him. She was disappointed and wished he had forgotten them.

John sat in his parked Cadillac and watched Edith and Bill enter the restaurant. His legs felt cramped and he got out of the car to stretch. He decided to take a little walk. He wondered what Edith was eating as he stood staring into a store window. He suddenly realized he was looking at women's underwear. He wanted to continue his walk, but didn't move. A black see-through negligee trimmed with feathers caught his eye.

John wanted Edith to have that negligee. He wondered if the store was still open. He tried the door. It was locked. "I must give Edith that negligee. I must give Edith that negligee." He said it over and over as he walked a few more blocks. His head moved in all directions, as if he was looking for something.

"This ought to do just fine," he said to himself, as he picked up a large stone from the side of the street.

He returned to the store and once again stared at the feathered negligee. Suddenly, and with all his might, he threw the stone at the glass storefront. It shattered easily. An alarm immediately began to screech in John's ears. He grabbed the negligee and ran as fast as he could. He got into his car and began to drive.

He was in a cold sweat and couldn't stop his body from shaking, but he was also elated. He steered his car recklessly, swerving in and out of the traffic. People swore at him, but he didn't hear. "I got away with it. I actually got away with it," he said. Stealing is a piece of cake, thought John. He couldn't wait to get home. He wanted to gift wrap the negligee he'd just stolen and leave it at Edith's door.

***

Edith and Bill were drinking their coffee. Dinner had been pleasant, but something was on Edith's mind. She could no longer restrain herself.

"I wonder if I'm jealous of that woman."

"What woman?"

"Liz whatever-her-name-is. The woman interviewing you."

Bill looked surprised.

"Why would you be jealous of her?"

"I don't know . . . She has a career, she seems assertive, and she seems to like you."

"So . . ."

"It annoys me."

"I don't think you're jealous. I just think you like acting like a child."

Bill's voice was harsh. Edith knew she should stop talking, but continued just the same.

"I guess if my life was more settled, it wouldn't bother me so much."

Bill looked at Edith and smiled.

"Bullshit. You and I both know there's a part of you that doesn't want to grow up."

Edith hated Bill at this moment. She couldn't tolerate being told what she felt or thought. Her anger surfaced.

"Look, don't tell me about my development. I work, I write. How dare you pass judgment on me?"

Bill remained calm.

"Edith, you said you might be jealous. I'm sorry if my opinion disturbed you. It was just an opinion. Take it for what it's worth. You don't have to defend your achievements to me. I'm with you because I respect and value you. Would you prefer it if I always agreed with you?"

Edith looked at him and smiled. "Maybe."

Bill answered her seriously, "Then you're with the wrong guy."

Edith's mind returned to John, Michel, all the men like them with whom she'd been. As each face passed in front of her, she felt a contraction in her stomach. To have been with them was so lonely. She took Bill's hand.

"I'm with the right guy, only sometimes it's hard for me to accept it."

Bill kissed her hand.

"Believe it or not, Edith, it's hard for me too. Let's leave it at that for now."

Edith again felt angry. What right did he have to end a discussion? This time she said nothing. She couldn't wait to finish her coffee and get out of there.

The weekend came and Bill announced that he was going to his friend's house. He wanted to write and worked better alone in the country. Edith had received no more notes, so neither she nor Bill felt as concerned as they had before. Edith convinced herself that she understood Bill's need to get away, and agreed that it was a good idea. Bill promised to call and encouraged her to do some work while he was gone.

With Bill out of town, Edith found herself restless. She decided to spend Saturday afternoon with Sarah. She arrived just as Sarah was getting into the shower. Paul was out for the day.

"Just make yourself comfortable. I'll be out in a minute."

Edith lay down on Sarah's bed. Within minutes she was asleep. When she finally opened her eyes, she saw Sarah fully dressed and reading a magazine on the opposite end of the bed.

"How long have I been sleeping?"

"About an hour."

"I'm exhausted. The tension of Bill, my work; I can't keep my eyes open."

"Then go back to sleep. I've plenty to do."

Edith barely heard Sarah's last words. She was already sleeping. The day continued that way. Edith got up, ate lunch, and went back to sleep. Finally it was time to go home.

"I'm sorry I was such poor company. I needed to unwind."

"Don't worry about it. I cleaned half the loft while you were sleeping."

"Good. Then I don't have to feel guilty."

Sarah kissed Edith good-bye and closed the door. Edith still felt slightly dazed as she made her way outside. It had begun to rain. She stood in the street looking for a taxi. A car passed. It suddenly stopped and backed up to where Edith stood.

"Edith?"

He was a familiar looking man.

"Hi, Michael Lance. A friend of John's."

Edith remembered who he was. She had met him on a few occasions when she was with John.

"If you don't mind coming with me to pick up a friend, I can give you a lift home. He lives nearby."

"Sure."

Michael wasn't really a close friend of John's. He was the sort of acquaintance that John liked having. If Edith remembered correctly, he produced records. She never did know how he and John had met and never cared. He was a stranger, but Edith was not about to say no to a ride home on a rainy evening. They picked up his friend and the three of them drove uptown. Edith turned her head to the backseat to introduce herself to Michael's friend.

"Edith Dorlen."

"Adam Lieber."

They shook hands, and in what seemed like a moment Edith was home.

"Would you like to have dinner with us?"

"I'd like to very much." She was happy Michael

had asked.

They drove downtown, crosstown, and uptown. It really didn't matter. Michael began passing around some cocaine, and the three of them partook freely. Each was in his own world. Soon they were all high. For Edith this was a novelty, and she allowed her body to abandon all the tension she hadn't known was there. Her body became so relaxed it felt limp. Michael continuously played tapes and the car became their sanctuary from the outside world. Edith broke the silence.

"I feel like we're in another country. It's so relaxing to be away from home."

Michael looked at her.

"I was thinking the same thing, but you ruined it by saying it."

His voice wasn't reproachful; he had merely made a comment. Edith felt no need to apologize. They finally got out of the car in Greenwich Village to find a place to eat. The rain had stopped and left the air fresh and cool. Adam stopped walking for a moment and spoke.

"Before we go to dinner, I want to show you people something."

He led Edith and Michael to a gate at the end of a small back street. There was a "No Trespassing" sign which Adam ignored as he swung open the gate. The three of them found themselves in a lovely courtyard filled with flowers and trees. Small houses surrounded the yard.

"Are we visiting someone here?" Edith inquired.

"No, I just thought you'd enjoy seeing this."

"It's real nice here Adam," Michael said to his friend. "I'm glad you took us."

Edith didn't appreciate the experience. She was hungry and felt a sudden attraction to Michael. They continued to walk and wandered into a small restaurant on Barrow Street. It was more like an old New England inn than a New York City restaurant.

Edith remembered herself as a little girl. She had gone to Barrow Street once a week for singing lessons. Whenever Edith arrived, her teacher would sneak a man out the back door. It occurred to Edith that she might have been doing more than just giving singing lessons.

"I guess it was hard for a woman to make money in those days," she said."

"What?" Michael thought he had missed something.

"Just thinking out loud."

The three of them were seated. Michael and Edith sat together on one side of the table. Adam sat across from them. Edith began to talk. She spoke of her short story that was soon to be published, the novel she was working on, the fact that she was getting older, and her beauty fading. As she spoke, she constantly ran her fingers through her hair. She was showing off, acting superior about her accomplishments, being nervous, and also trying to be seductive. In between sentences Michael offered her rolls. Edith just shook her head and kept talking. She suddenly stopped.

"I'm sorry. It's either the dope or nervousness

which has made me talk so much."

"I liked listening," said Michael, as he offered Edith the crust from a piece of rye bread. He had buttered it especially for her.

"How did you know that's just what I love?"

Michael smiled, "Just a guess. My kids love it too. I really love my kids."

Edith was surprised to hear that Michael had children and wondered if he was married.

"Sometimes it pains me," he continued, "I love them so much."

Edith gave him a knowing look.

"Do you think the pain is for them, or for yourself?"

Adam's presence got lost for the moment.

"I guess a little of both. This conversation is getting too heavy for one night away from the world."

Michael would go so far, but no further. Edith was disappointed. He became less interesting to her. They finished dinner and returned to the car. They snorted more cocaine and off they went. Edith closed her eyes and listened to the music. Michael touched her hand. She felt as if they were making love. Suddenly the car stopped. Edith opened her eyes. They were at the boat basin on the West Side. No one spoke as they got out of the car and walked to the water. Everything was very still. No one was in sight. Edith could already see the headlines in the morning papers. THREE NEW YORKERS KILLED AT BOAT BASIN ON WEST SIDE.

"Let's go back to the car. I feel frightened."

Michael put his arm around her.

"There's nothing to be afraid of. Only monkeys and elephants come here at night."

"I still want to go."

They returned to the car. Edith suddenly got angry.

"I felt so good in my own world and you had to stop the car and ruin it for me."

"We'll get you back into it," Adam's voice spoke from the backseat. "Relax, you'll go back."

Edith did return to her private ecstasy. At three o'clock in the morning Michael stopped the car in front of her building. Edith vaguely remembered having said good night to Adam.

"Would you like to come in?" Edith wanted to make love.

"No, some other time, but not tonight. It's late."

Edith got out of the car and walked around to Michael's side. She bent her head to meet his and kissed him. He remained passive. She kissed him again and walked inside her building.

"I wonder what I was doing with them?" thought Edith as she opened her front door. She lay in bed and thought about her behavior. She'd had a nice evening. Both men had been kind but she couldn't leave it at that. She had wanted to sleep with Michael and wondered why.

"Is it Bill's absence? Insecurity, insurance? Do I need a backup team to be able to love? Maybe I'm still spiting John."

Whatever it was, she knew she'd regressed and felt slightly ashamed. God, growing up was truly *très difficile.*

***

John had his secretary buy him an empty gift box and some pink ribbon during her lunch hour. She thought it odd, but then she'd found his entire behavior odd over the last few months. Most of the time he didn't take calls and stayed locked in his office. She didn't say anything because her job had become so easy, but it was also getting boring. She didn't really think she was needed anymore.

John waited patiently for her to return. The sheer negligee was in his attache case just waiting to be wrapped. There'd been hardly any room for his papers when he'd left that morning.

"I'll leave it at her door this evening," he thought. "I'll put a note in with it."

He sat down at his large desk, took a sheet of paper from his memo pad, and began to write. He heard his secretary knock at the door and got up to open it. After walking a few paces, he returned to his desk and slipped the sheet of paper under his large Mark Cross blotter. He quickly walked to the door and opened it.

"I hope this is what you wanted," said his secretary, handing him the box.

"Where's the ribbon?"

"I put it inside the box."

"That's fine. Perfect. Thank you."

He quickly dismissed her and relocked his door.

"I love it. I love it." He was placing the negligee inside the box. He removed the paper from beneath the blotter and finished writing his note. He began to whistle as he placed the ribbon around the box. "She'll really love this," he thought. "I wish I could see her face when she opens it. Oh God, I'm hungry."

John buzzed his secretary and ordered a large lunch.

***

Edith opened her front door to go out. Bill had just returned from the country and she was going to his apartment to see him. She almost tripped over a box which was resting in front of her door. "What the hell is this?" she thought as she picked it up. She immediately sat down and opened it. Her eyes looked disbelievingly at the negligee. She didn't want to pick it up or touch it. A note, written in red ink, caught her eye. That she picked up and read.

SORRY YOU NEVER WORE THIS WITH ME. POOR GIRL. YOUR NEW BOYFRIEND DOESN'T STAY IN TOWN WEEKENDS. YOU'LL HAVE TO PUT IT ON FOR HIM DURING THE WEEK. TELL HIM A GAZELLE SENT IT TO YOU. ARE YOU STILL A CUNT? . . . YOU'LL ALWAYS BE A

CUNT. . . CUNT . . . CUNT.

Edith threw the paper on the floor. She was almost certain that John was the one tormenting her. This knowledge made her feel sick. She wondered if she should call him and tell him she knew. Her hand reached for the note. She put it into her bag and left the apartment.

"I think I'll take a bus."

Edith needed to feel the presence of other people around her.

***

Bill sat looking at the note.

"Do you want me to call him?"

Edith shook her head. "I'm not even sure it's him," she said nervously.

"Well, either way, you've got nothing to lose by asking."

"He seems to have become so crazy, I don't know what he'd do. I think the best thing is to ignore him. I don't think he'd ever admit it anyway."

"Then you should go to the police."

"They would never believe an upstanding tycoon like John was guilty of anything, except perhaps stealing."

"Stay with me here tonight."

Edith looked at Bill and smiled. "I'd love to."

***

The two of them were in bed together. Bill gently stroked Edith's hair. Her body was still filled with apprehension over John. She couldn't shake the nauseated feeling his note had left inside her. Bill smiled. His face wore a kind expression and his eyes sparkled with warmth and affection. He placed his fingers on her crotch and slowly began to rub it. At first he touched it lightly, then suddenly thrust one of his fingers as far up inside her as it could go. He continued this motion, exciting Edith more and more. She wanted to touch him but instead lay very still, soaking in the pleasure she was feeling. She knew he wouldn't stop until she wanted him inside her.

His other hand caressed her breast. He made her nipple hard and then sucked on it with his mouth. She was becoming hotter and hotter. Bill's fingers responded to her heat by moving faster and faster. He wanted Edith to have an orgasm. He'd continue to give her pleasure until she was satisfied.

Suddenly Edith felt afraid. Maybe he's loving me just to trap me. Then he'll throw me out, she thought. Her vagina became dry. Bill acted as if he didn't notice and used the saliva from his mouth to wet her again. Edith looked at him. He was now moving his tongue in and out of her. She watched him make love to her and realized she really loved him. Edith let out a huge sigh that never seemed to end.

It was the most complete orgasm she'd ever had. Bill held her in his arms without saying a word. They both rested. As Edith lay there she greatly desired to give Bill the pleasure he'd just given her. She wanted to be good to him without expecting anything in return particularly, she just wanted to give to him. No more balancing out the ledger: you do this for me and I'll do that for you. She felt none of that. In fact, she felt nothing but a strong desire to make Bill happy.

She touched his prick and found it hard. She stroked it gently with her hands. Bill gave out small cries of pleasure. He was suddenly on top of her and in a matter of moments she felt him inside. He moved in and out slowly, and with complete control. Edith quickly became wet again. They moved from one position to another. He always remained inside of her. She was on top of him, by his side, and then he turned her on her stomach. Edith got up on her knees and felt him get harder and harder. She knew if she felt like hitting him, he wouldn't mind. He wanted to feel it all. She sat up on her knees. He was still behind her and held her waist tightly. He remained inside of her.

Edith spoke. "I want to hit you with my fists for making me fall in love with you. I also want to lick your entire body lovingly with my tongue, and for the same reason."

Bill laughed and gently pushed her body back under his. As he moved in and out of her, his hand stroked her ass.

"We'll have fun together, Edith. We'll do everything."

He bent over her and squeezed her breast with one of his hands. Edith became so excited the room began to spin.

They both came. Edith believed that Bill had poured his entire insides into her. Their bodies stayed locked together until the beat of their hearts slowed down. Then they lay side by side and held hands. Soon they were asleep.

Bill handed Edith her morning cup of coffee and sat down beside her. He had put vanilla ice cream in the coffee instead of cream and sugar. Edith loved it that way.

As she licked the melted ice cream from around her lips, she spoke. "I've often wondered why some people who write the most beautiful music, paint the greatest paintings, express the most profound thoughts, are in real life ugly."

Bill was quiet for a moment and then answered.

"Maybe they're giving you the best parts of themselves through their art. I never like to meet anyone who's work I respect. They're bound to disappoint me. I've met people who's work is mediocre and most of the time find them very human. It's a big mistake to confuse the person with his work."

"I guess you're right," Edith answered pensively, "only I wish it weren't so."

"Why?"

"I don't know," Edith shrugged. "I just wish it weren't so."

Bill spoke softly. "My father was a great writer, but a miserable person."

Edith thought she saw a flicker of pain cross

Bill's face. Her hand reached for his. They sat quietly for some moments. Edith knew she loved this man and wanted to be with him. She suddenly felt a deep commitment to their relationship. "No one ever died from a broken heart," she thought.

"I am not helpless, I am not helpless," Edith said aloud.

Bill looked at Edith with surprise.

"Where did that come from?"

"My gut."

"Well, if you want to talk about helplessness, I'd say you were a pretty tough woman who sometimes prefers feeling weak and small. Helpless you're not, baby."

Bill put down his coffee cup and lit a cigarette. He gave it to Edith and lit another one for himself. She continued speaking.

"I have to learn to believe more in myself and my work."

Bill disagreed.

"Just from observing you, I'd say you have a certain self-conceit. Feeling helpless is your convenient excuse for lack of commitment. What did you do this weekend, Edith? I tried calling you Saturday night and no one answered."

Edith was caught off guard. She wondered if it was necessary to tell him the truth. Saturday night had been meaningless. She felt that there were times when honesty was cruel and unnecessary. Maybe this was one of those times. She was slow in answering, but Edith found herself unable to lie.

"I accidentally met a man I know very slightly and went to dinner with him and his friend. We ate and drove around the city in his car. That's it."

"Did you go with them because you felt helpless without me here or because you wanted to be with them?"

"I'm not sure."

"I suggest you find out. It's important."

Edith put out her cigarette and placed her head in Bill's lap.

"I love you."

Bill looked down at her lovely face.

"You're scared right now. Tell me that when you don't feel frightened and I'll believe you."

Edith smiled and closed her eyes. Bill caressed her face with his hand. He too was in love.

Edith left Bill's apartment. The air outside was clear and the sun was shining. She decided to walk and found herself in the midst of an Italian block party. She watched the vendors selling their wares on the street. Then she turned her attention to her surroundings. There was a carnival atmosphere in the air. Stall after stall was filled with displays of religious objects: Jesus hanging from the cross, the Virgin Mary, and various porcelain saints who wore expressions of faith under suffering. Colored crepe paper streamers hung from lampposts. A man bumped into her by accident. He wore a T-shirt that read Kiss Me I'm Italian. "Why doesn't he look where he's going," Edith muttered under her breath.

Suddenly Edith became strangely uncomfortable, as if someone was watching her. She looked around. There, in a crowd by a vegetable stand, she saw two dark brown eyes boring into her. "God, it looks like John." She became frightened and turned her head away. "I must be imagining things. Stay very still and look again." She looked once more at the vegetable stand, but the eyes were gone. "So what if it was John," she rationalized. Nevertheless she began walking in the other direction.

A woman selling fabrics caught her eye and Edith approached her stall. As she fingered the various cotton prints she once more felt uneasy, but this time was afraid to look away from the bolts of cloth. They all blurred. The polka dots mixed with the stripes, the yellows with the greens, and she could barely hear the voice of the little Italian lady when she asked if she could be of some help. Edith just shook her head without daring to look up. Finally she regained control of herself and walked away from the stall.

She moved her legs at a normal pace but some irrational feeling forced her to turn her head around. There he was directly behind her, his dark eyes staring right through her, a small smile on his lips. He had his dog with him on a leash. This time Edith knew she wasn't imagining him and she ran into the middle of the street. Cars began honking their horns but she didn't care. A taxi finally appeared and she ran the length of the block to get into it. Edith breathed a sigh of relief as she closed the taxi door and leaned back in the seat. But she still couldn't erase John's eyes from her mind. She was now certain he was the one sending her the lewd notes. She also knew he wanted to kill her.

***

Sarah and Paul decided on a temporary separation. She would move into the Chelsea Hotel by the weekend. Paul sat with his wife and spoke.

"Our energy level is so low, Sarah. We're hurting each other too much. I sometimes feel like I'm having a nervous breakdown, or am on the verge of killing myself."

Sarah couldn't bear to see Paul suffer this way. Somewhere she felt responsible for her mother's suicide, which produced great feelings of pity and remorse in her for her husband. She also knew she'd dragged him down with her. The only way to spare him more grief was to leave. She knew Nicholas was out of her life, even though she'd now be free to be with him again. No way out. Sarah would have to be alone. In a way she welcomed the opportunity. It was a chance to grow, work, and develop on her own. There were no thoughts of other men. What she and Paul really needed at the moment was to find two good jobs. Sarah would start looking immediately. She hoped Paul wasn't too distracted and depressed to do the same.

The move to the Chelsea wasn't as painful as Sarah had imagined it would be. Paul remained home. The experience of checking in at the desk and going to her room felt like a dream. The first thing Sarah did was call Paul. "I'm here."

Paul paused. "Maybe you should come home." His voice was choked with emotion.

They both hung up their phones in tears.

Sarah calmed down and took a sketch pad from her suitcase. She began to draw. She hadn't done any drawing in years, but felt the urge to do so now. When she was finished she found the paper filled with sketched hands. Some were old and wrinkled, others had long tapered fingers, and one or two were the size of a baby's. Sarah enjoyed looking at her work and fell asleep thinking of hands.

A few days later Sarah received a letter from her poet friend at the Zen Center. He said everyone missed her, including roshi. This flattered Sarah. The thought of so spiritual a man even remembering her was a great compliment. The Chelsea was getting boring. It was too funky for Sarah, and with Paul so nearby the temptation to return home was indeed great. The Zen Center might be the perfect place to go. It would put a lot of distance between her unsuccessful past and precarious present. California, Mount Woods, space, all seemed very attractive to Sarah right now. She decided to call Edith and ask her to have dinner with her. She was anxious to hear her friend's opinion on the subject.

Bill answered the phone. Edith quickly took the

receiver from him and spoke to Sarah. Her voice had a nervous edge to it.

"Is anything the matter, Edith?" Sarah asked.

"No, nothing really."

"What's Bill doing there during your writing hours?"

Sarah was teasing her friend. Edith answered simply.

"He's moved in with me for a while."

Sarah again thought Edith sounded nervous but imagined it was possibly because Bill was there.

"I thought you might want to come to the hotel and have dinner with me tonight."

Edith asked her to hold on a moment and covered the receiver while she spoke to Bill. Sarah wondered what all the secrecy was about.

"I'll be there around seven," said Edith.

"Great. See you then."

***

Bill put Edith into a taxi and told her he would pick her up at the Chelsea at eleven o'clock. Since Edith's latest experience with John had frightened her so much, Bill insisted on staying with her. She hadn't resisted him at all. Edith didn't want to alarm Sarah about John, so she never mentioned his crazy antics to her. She was glad to be having dinner with Sarah this evening.

The two women walked into the Chelsea dining room and were quickly seated. Sarah waved hello to a few people.

"You seem right at home."

"I am, but it's claustrophobic and safe. It's true that I've done some nice work here. I'm drawing again and enjoy it."

"Are you drawing anything special?"

"Hands."

"I'd like to see what you've done."

"Okay, maybe after dinner."

"Is there any particular reason for just drawing hands?"

"It makes me feel peaceful."

Edith didn't respond to her friend's statement, instead she looked at the menu. There was something about hotels that always gave Edith pleasure. She was happy Sarah had invited her there for dinner. She didn't want to talk about John and risk becoming depressed and frightened.

They ordered, and Sarah then decided to tell her friend of her plans.

"I was thinking of returning to California, to the Zen Center."

Edith looked surprised. "Why?"

"I'm tired of thinking. I want to discover my spiritual side."

"But Sarah, you've never thought."

Sarah laughed.

"Of course you're right. What I mean is I'm tired of wondering about my marriage, Nicholas, and so forth. I felt clean at the Center."

Edith knew what that meant and how important it was.

"When were you planning to leave?"

"Probably next week."

Edith felt numb. Sarah looked at Edith and smiled.

"You'll come to visit me there."

"I'll be all right. It's just that intimate ties are difficult to form when you're forty. Everyone comes with a history and it's a bore to try to explain who you are. God, I'll miss you, Sarah. I hope this move of yours is only temporary."

Sarah placed her hand on Edith's.

"Right now it's the only option I have. Who knows, in a few months I may be back."

They both felt sad and once more Sarah felt she brought sadness to everyone she loved.

After dinner Sarah took Edith back to her room to see her drawings. Edith liked the various types of hands Sarah had drawn.

"They're interesting. I can see how they could be comforting as well."

Sarah smiled broadly. She was proud of her work and had enjoyed doing it.

"You want a drink or something?"

"No thanks. Bill's picking me up in the lobby at eleven o'clock."

Sarah looked at Edith. She knew Edith wasn't telling her something, but didn't want to pry. Maybe they already knew too many of each other's secrets.

"You're lucky to have him."

"I know it. He's a nice person. Thanks for dinner, Sarah. I'll call you tomorrow."

They kissed each other good-bye and Edith was gone. Sarah looked around her room and wondered if a change in geography could alter her life. She hoped it could, but was finding it more and more difficult to believe in miracles.

Bill had moved into Edith's apartment after her encounter with John on the street. She welcomed his presence. John had unnerved her and she didn't want to be alone.

After returning from the Chelsea with Bill, Edith went directly to her bedroom. She washed and got into bed, expecting Bill to do the same. He entered the bedroom and seemed just to want to talk. Edith was shocked when he kissed her good night and went into the living room. He had been working while she was visiting Sarah and apparently saw no reason to stop. Edith knew that Bill required space of his own. It was difficult for her to accept his need for privacy without feeling rejected. She was hurt when he left her and followed him into the living room, wanting some explanation for being left by herself. He was putting sheets on the living room couch when Edith entered the room. It was hard for her to understand how he could possibly not want to be with her when she wanted so much to be with him.

"Don't you love me?"

Bill looked up at Edith standing in the middle of the room.

"I love you very much, but some nights I like to

sleep alone. I don't know how late I'll be working and don't want to worry about it. There will be a time when you'll want the same. I'll respect your wish and not feel hurt. In fact, I'd probably realize how much you loved me. Do you know why?"

Edith shook her head.

"Because you'd be doing what you wanted to do and you'd know I understood. I'd like you to try to understand me now. I need to work and sleep alone tonight and if you try and deprive me of that, I'll resent it. If you understand, I'll appreciate it."

He left Edith no choice and she returned to her room. She thought about what he had said and tried to bury her hurt feelings. Edith wanted to understand about commitment, and how it didn't always mean two people wanting to do the same thing at the same time. It dawned on her that true generosity and consideration allow people to have different wants and needs, and that that was all right. What a relief it was to finally understand this, Edith thought. She knew she'd have to work constantly with herself on these ideas, since she had never really understood these things, and her family certainly hadn't provided her with examples. "Yes, I'll really have to work on all this." Her eyes closed and she finally fell asleep.

The next day Bill was as loving as ever. On a few other occasions, he wanted to be alone, and Edith was learning to accept it better each time. He was proving to her that they could be separate and yet together. She felt a little like the child who goes to school for the first time and spends each day wondering if her mother will be there when she returns home. Only after seeing day after day that she is home does the child begin to trust being away from her.

John knew that Bill had moved in with Edith and it enraged him. He decided not to go to work for at least two afternoons a week, hoping in this way to catch her alone. He suspected that Bill wouldn't always be with her during the day. He would watch her apartment and wait for one of them to leave. John now carried his gun with him at all times.

As he made his way to Edith's apartment, he squinted his eyes at all the familiar faces that passed by him. He suddenly stopped in front of a middle-aged woman. The woman looked at him and smiled politely.

"Wipe that grin off your face, mother."

The woman's face registered surprise.

"I'm sorry. You must have made some mistake."

She began to walk away quickly. John caught her by the shoulder from behind.

"Trying to get away from me, mother? My, my, mother, you sure have gained weight."

The woman shrugged off his arm and walked into a store. John stood outside, still screaming at her.

"You're a goddamn whore, mother, a goddamn whore!"

After that, he quieted down and stuck his tongue out at her. The people in the store decided that the world was no longer a fit place to live in when such a well-dressed looking gentleman behaved in such a fashion.

John continued on his way. He wondered what his mother was doing in New York. He forgot that she'd been dead for twenty-seven years. John took his usual spying post and waited. He hoped that Bill would come out alone so that he could trap Edith in her apartment. His vigil paid off. John watched Bill get on a crosstown bus. He crossed the street and entered the lobby of Edith's building. He already knew how to get past the doorman, having done it so many times before. He simply waited for someone to distract the man and then walked directly to the elevator. He made sure to move at a normal pace, not wanting to attract attention to himself. The elevator doors opened and John walked directly to Edith's apartment and rang the bell.

Edith had just sat down at her desk to write when she was startled by the sound of the door bell. "I wonder who that is," she thought. She stood up from her chair and walked slowly to the door. "Maybe Bill forgot his keys."

"Who's there?"

"It's me."

Edith didn't really pay close attention to the voice that had answered her. She just assumed it was Bill. Edith opened her double-locked door and found herself staring at John. He had a large grin on his face.

"Aren't you going to invite me in, Edith?"

She stood there, too surprised to understand

what she should do. John simply walked through the open door and locked it behind him.

Edith quickly regained control of herself and decided to be very polite, even gentle. They had once been lovers. She didn't believe he would hurt her.

"Sit down, John."

As they sat across from one another, Edith smiled at him. She was struck by his haggard appearance, and almost felt sorry for him. "No, he'd never hurt me," she thought. Her mind suddenly flashed back to the time John had anally raped her. He had hurt her then. He'd wanted total submission, and the night he raped her she had fought him, but he had won. A chill ran down her spine. She had forgotten that incident until this moment.

"Did you like the nightgown I got you?"

Edith was surprised by his blatant admission.

"Yes, thank you very much."

"Did your boyfriend like it?"

Edith tried to change the subject. "Can I get you something to drink, John?"

John moved his body to the edge of the couch and squinted his eyes until they almost disappeared.

"I said, did your boyfriend like it?"

"Yes. He thought it was very nice."

Edith was silently praying that Bill would quickly return. She realized John was crazy. John watched her from the corner of his eye. He offered Edith a cigarette. She took it and remained seated.

"It's too bad you betrayed me because you were a

good fuck."

Edith said nothing. She was both angry and frightened. She knew she might give off negative vibrations if she spoke. Sweat began to trickle down her body and it took all her control to stop her hands from shaking. She thought it best for her to remain silent until she felt in control of herself. She smoked her cigarette and listened to his voice. John suddenly stood up and walked to Edith's chair. He began to rub her back. She remained motionless.

"Why don't you come stay with me? We can travel together. I know you love to travel. You'll take care of me. In return, I'll fuck you to death. It will be good between us, exciting. I promise you that you'll never be bored."

Edith decided to play along with him, not wanting to provoke him into any violence.

"It sounds good to me," she said. Her voice was lighthearted.

"It will be," he answered seriously.

She realized he was being truthful at this moment. He continued to stroke her back as she sat like a statue.

"If ever I had to leave you, I'd send a lesbian to make love to you and keep you happy until I was there."

Edith realized that as long as he was talking, she was safe. This prompted her to keep him going.

"Why send me a woman, why not a man?"

"That would make me too jealous. You belong to me." His hand was now gently stroking her hair.

"Sounds great," she answered.

"Oh, come on, Edith. You could do a lot worse than me."

He walked in front of her and began to pose and ripple his muscles.

"My body's in terrific shape. I'd fuck you every night. What more could you ask for? Have you ever been with a man that can fuck you the way I do?"

"Maybe once or twice."

Edith said those words teasingly, hoping to keep John talking. He smiled and dropped his pose.

"If they were that good, you'd still be with them. I know you, Edith. I know what you need. I know this fag you're with now is just temporary. That's why I'm not jealous."

Edith felt nothing but loathing and disgust. John returned to Edith and suddenly pulled her hair viciously back. It hurt and she tried to remove his hand from her head. But he grabbed it tighter. It was his way of trying to seduce and bully her at the same time. Once more, she decided not to fight him.

"I'm just teasing you, John. You know I'd go anywhere with you, do anything you want. You've always made me feel so feminine. When we made love, didn't I submit myself totally to you?"

He finally let go of her hair. She felt dizzy but managed to smile. Her smile frustrated him. He wanted her to be in real pain.

"I want you to get rid of that guy you're with and come with me. I'll give you a week. If this isn't settled by then, I'm going to kill somebody. I'm always watching, so don't try anything. See what I have here?"

He pulled the gun out of the inside of his jacket pocket.

"It's real; it works."

Remain calm, she thought, remain calm . . . calm . . . calm. Edith lit another cigarette and spoke.

"You can count on me, John. I'll come to you in a week."

She wondered if he believed her. She couldn't be sure, but suspected he did. Edith knew he wanted to believe her and saw her as his female counterpart. She may have once been. She looked at him, saw his madness, and felt totally degraded. She almost wished he'd kill her. He suddenly walked to the door and opened it.

"I'll expect you in a week. Remember, between the sexes, it's always who kills whom first."

He slammed the door behind him.

***

Bill finally returned. He found Edith in bed, saw her tearstained face and knew she'd been crying. He sat down on the bed and stroked Edith's face. Tears streamed down from her eyes and touched Bill's hand. He didn't try to stop her from crying.

"Do you want to tell me what happened?"

His voice was quiet, kind. Edith turned her head away from him as if she was ashamed. Bill waited. The words poured out of her like a faucet, giving him every detail of John's visit. Bill said nothing. Instead, he took Edith into his arms and rocked her, trying to soothe her body and mind. She continued to speak.

"Do you hate me?"

Bill looked down at her cradled in his arms and shook his head.

"Why should I hate you?"

"I hate myself for ever having been involved with him. When he left I took a bath and washed myself over and over. He made me feel so dirty."

Bill smiled at her. "None of us is a saint, Edith."

He released her from his arms, stood up and undressed. His naked body slid under the covers, next to Edith's. He wanted to love Edith. He knew it was important to help her wipe away John and every other man she'd been with. His tongue caressed every opening in her body. She felt every orifice opening up, waiting to receive him. Her body was relieved not to hold anything back. Edith had more pleasure now than ever before in her life. Bill wanted her to have it, and so she took it, and returned it with all her heart. Nothing about his body repulsed her. She even loved the hole in his ass and desired to lick it and finger it for hours. His hands, lips, prick were all exploring her.

"What are you looking for?" Her voice came from the darkening room.

"I'm looking for the flashes of color in you that make you so beautiful to me."

Edith loved him for accepting her so fully. She licked every inch of his body with her tongue, loving the way his body shivered with pleasure. Their lovemaking continued on and off for hours. They finally stopped and rested next to one another.

"I have an idea," Bill said.

"What?"

"How would you like me to cook us some spaghetti? I think we both could use some nourishment right now."

"Umm, I'd love it."

"Good."

He got out of bed to go to the kitchen.

"You just rest and relax. I want to bring it to you in bed." With that, he disappeared.

Bill was spoiling her when she needed to be spoiled and Edith loved it. His generous spirit was helping to ease the pain of John. Bill was preparing her to be able to deal with John practically. He returned with two plates of spaghetti and some wine on a tray. They both sat naked in bed eating their late night snack.

"This is so perfect. I don't think anything ever tasted so good to me."

Bill laughed delightedly, knowing he'd gotten Edith's mind off John. The day had been tense. They were both grateful to be close to one another. They finished eating and finally fell asleep for a few hours. Edith's last thought before closing her eyes was that she'd forgotten to call Sarah. I'll do it tomorrow, and find out if she's really leaving.

***

Sarah was picked up at the airport by her old college friend Carol. She had only seen her briefly on her last trip to California, but was delighted to feel happy upon seeing her again. Carol had always been somewhat of an enigma to Sarah. In public she was loud and competitive. Privately, Sarah found her understanding and capable of being intimate. They could talk together the way she and Edith always had. Sometimes, Sarah thought she was even more understanding than Edith, knowing Sarah's needs for the Japanese roshi and meditation. Edith sometimes poo-pooed Sarah's Eastern side, calling it a cop-out, but Sarah knew Carol would welcome her into her home for a few days and would take her to the Zen Center when she was ready to go.

Carol drove Sarah back to her house along the Los Angeles freeways. Sarah was happy to be there. There were no distractions or pressures to cope with, and, thank God, no immediate decisions to be made. Discussions of affairs, separations, were all left back in cluttered New York.

Carol acted in films a little, and had an income of her own which provided her with a decent lifestyle. Her house was California bungalow style, the kind often found close to the ocean. It was in Los Feliz. Sarah immediately loved it and knew she had made the right choice in going west.

Carol helped Sarah unpack her clothes and went

to great lengths to admire them. The two women were getting reacquainted, but it was not difficult. That night they barbecued steaks for their dinner and tried to catch up on each other's lives. When Sarah finished talking about herself, she fully realized how little had happened. It was true she was now a full editor and could make a living on her own, but she realized her small film was very important to her. If she could uncloud her mind enough to make another one in California, she'd be happy. Carol described her life in her rather energized crackling voice. Sarah listened and realized just how unglamorous life could be: Broken love affairs, acting jobs almost gotten, disappointments with friends. Carol had gone through it all, retained her good humor, and most certainly her sense of survival.

Carol's kitchen had so many utensils hanging from the walls that Sarah was convinced she was a gourmet cook.

"You must really spend time in the kitchen," remarked Sarah, looking around her.

"Oh no, everyone in California has this shit. Out here it's the look of things, not the reality. After a while you forget what's real or unreal. For about a week I really thought I could cook, but then I tasted what I was preparing and realized it was the same crap I always made. The utensils even had me fooled. Now I just think of them as decorations and realize they haven't changed my cooking at all."

Sarah laughed at Carol's clarity and hoped some of it would rub off on her.

Carol made an appointment for the two women to visit the Disney Studios. Sarah loved special effects and remembered discussing them with Edith. She could still hear Edith's voice as she dressed herself to go.

"Sarah, sometimes they're an excuse for no content. When you think of something that takes your breath away, it was Esther Williams diving into the deep water and surfacing with a gorgeous smile on her face, or Sonja Henie twirling on the ice in a magnificent skater's costume. Those weren't special effects. They were human beings thrilling us. Sharks, devils, earthquakes, fires, robots, that's special effects. I think it's boring and dehumanizing."

Sarah recalled her response. She had agreed with Edith but said she always preferred working without too much thought. Her friend's response still rang in her ears.

"It's time for changes, Sarah. You might as well begin dealing with your intellect. You might even like it. If you know what you're thinking, feeling, doing, at least you're in control."

As Sarah and Carol left the house, Sarah hoped she wouldn't be too seduced by what she saw. She knew Edith's words were as true of life as of work.

***

Edith and Bill walked into the police station. They had both decided that it was time to tell the police what was going on. Edith wanted them to know she was being watched by John and that he carried a gun.

The precinct was different from what Edith had expected. It had yellow walls that looked like they needed a good plastering. The fluorescent lights reflected the yellow surrounding them, giving off an eerie light. A policeman stopped them at the door and asked them what they wanted. Bill briefly explained, and they were told to go upstairs. They walked up a wooden staircase and sat down on an old wooden bench. The lighting was the same upstairs as it was downstairs. Policemen laughed and talked together as they walked back and forth from one room to another. Edith felt odd sitting there, but she was not at all distressed by it. She was rather intrigued with these men who were the upholders of the law.

After waiting about ten minutes, a black mustached policeman invited them into a small office and told them to sit down. He asked the nature of their problem. Edith showed him two of the notes she'd received and told him of the visit John had made to her.

"He threatened me."

"In what way," asked the policeman.

"He said he'd kill someone if I didn't go back to him in a week."

The policeman listened sympathetically.

"There isn't really much the police can do in this matter. We can talk to him, but he'll probably deny everything. Until he actually does something illegal, we can't arrest the guy or even bother him."

Edith was disgusted.

"You mean he has to kill me before you can do anything?"

The policeman didn't respond to her question. Bill tried to be helpful by asking a question of his own.

"Do you have any advice for us?"

The policeman looked at him and nodded his head. "The best thing you can do is ignore him. He's looking for attention. If he calls, hang up on him or change your phone number. Neither of you should answer the door for anyone and the lady here shouldn't go out alone."

"Well, he hasn't called yet," said Edith.

"That may start. In these cases, vulgarity and threats very often come over the telephone."

"If he feels frustrated enough," said Bill, "that may come next."

"He's already done all that," said Edith. Her tone was sarcastic. The policeman didn't seem to notice, and continued to speak.

"You said you used to date this guy. Am I correct?"

"Yes," answered Edith, feeling disconsolate.

"Then your doorman must know him. Tell him to keep his eyes open."

Bill took Edith's hand and they both stood up. The three of them knew it was a fruitless visit. The cop felt bad. He wished he could be more helpful.

"Look, you can press charges against this guy

and we can follow it up, but my advice is to ignore him. We patrol your street pretty regularly. If he's there often enough maybe we can get him for loitering."

Edith shrugged her shoulders, knowing that no cop would dare accuse rich John of loitering. It would do no good anyhow. In fact, for the moment there was nothing anyone could do. The policeman took a business card from his pocket and handed it to Edith.

"I had these made up when I did a little acting in a movie. Give me a call if anything else happens but I can't promise much."

He extended his hand to Edith and Bill and shook their hands firmly. He then walked them to the door. They left the police station feeling helpless and depressed.

John watched them from his Cadillac and was furious that Edith had dared to go to the police. "That lying cunt. She said she'd come to me and now she's talking to the police. She's asking for it. No more presents from me. She's asking for it."

John returned to his office, whisked by his secretary, and locked his door. He sat down behind his large desk, tapped on the blotter with his fingertips, and stared at the telephone.

Edith and Bill entered the apartment to the sound of the telephone ringing. Edith picked up the receiver while Bill locked the door. They had spoken to the doorman who denied having seen John since Edith stopped going with him.

"Hello." Edith's voice was slightly breathless.

"It's too bad you betrayed me because you were a

good fuck."

Edith motioned Bill over to her and held the receiver into the air so that the two of them could listen.

"I'd like you to blow me right now and then I'd throw you out, you worthless bitch."

Before Edith could say a word, he hung up. Edith and Bill looked at each other despairingly.

"I guess that cop knew what he was talking about. We'll have to change your number."

"God, it's a nightmare."

Bill could think of nothing comforting to say. He made the two of them lunch, which neither of them ate, and sat down to do some work. He suggested that Edith should try to do the same. Edith agreed but continued to sit and stare into space. Bill left her alone.

The calls continued. Once the phone rang in the middle of the night. Edith and Bill were awake. They were both too restless to sleep.

"Do you think I should answer it?" asked Edith. There was fear in her voice.

"You might as well. He'll keep it up until you do."

Edith picked up the receiver. They both could hear his angry voice.

"I'm going to kill the both of you. The lying whore and her lover will be buried together," John hissed venomously.

As soon as John hung up Edith took the phone off the hook. She and Bill both got to the point of never wanting to touch a telephone. Edith felt like pulling it out of the wall. She thanked God her number would be changed the following morning.

***

Edith needn't have bothered changing her number. When John entered his office the next morning, he was informed by his lawyer that he was being indicted by the SEC. John's conglomerate and some of its officials were accused of various illegalities. John had known it was coming but felt incapable of stopping it. It was like his madness, out of control. His life didn't mean much to him anymore and neither did his reputation. He and his company had been buying worthless swamp land and inflating the value and monetary worth in the annual stock reports. John was the one who had originally worked out this scheme, but he hadn't had much trouble convincing his associates to go along with him. To justify the swindle, he'd rationalized by saying he was merely using the newest accounting techniques. "Everyone does it," he'd said.

If he hadn't totally lost his mind and been able to watch his business, he might have avoided the law. But that was not the case, and it was just a matter of time before he got caught. Yet feeling so rich and powerful, he thought nobody would dare touch him. As usual he was one step removed from reality and the temper of the times.

Corruption was out of fashion this year, but John was too insulated and removed from the norm to know it. John and his associates immediately denied any wrongdoings, and were willing to swear to their honesty, but these were stalling tactics. If one of them broke, they would all go down. John's lawyer informed him that one of his coconspirators was already informing in exchange for a lighter sentence.

John told his lawyer to handle things as best he could and left his office. He was in agony as he walked the streets aimlessly, stopping every now and then to stare at what he believed to be a familiar face. He felt pains in his head when he thought about the exposure and public humiliation that was in store for him. The world would see him naked and find him wanting. "Hang tough" was the corporate lingo used in situations like this. It had no meaning for him now, though in the past he remembered using that expression to nervous employees. He couldn't bear walking any more, his legs felt like two deadweights under him. He hailed a passing taxi and went home.

The first thing he did when he entered his apartment was to take the phone off the hook. No reporters. No lawyers. After making himself a double martini, he lay down on his couch to think. His mind was clearer now than it had been for a long time. John realized his whole life had been lived to protect who he was and now he knew why. It's hard to admit to having a criminal mentality, so up until this moment he never had.

"I wish I could get rid of the pain in my head," he said aloud.

As the day went by, John sat alone sipping his martinis. He had never felt so alone in his life. Tears streamed down his face when he realized he had no one to call in his hour of need. There was no reserve of good feelings left over for him from any of his relationships. Edith was gone and his partner was no longer involved with him. His ex-wife certainly couldn't be counted on. He had himself and his dog. It was a grim situation. The value of caring was to be cared for in return. John's money had found its way into people's pockets but not their hearts. The rich man was now bankrupt. His clean money had turned dirty and no one wanted to touch it anymore. It was as if the virgin had turned whore.

He banged his head with his fists, trying to relieve the pain he felt. Finally everything ceased to exist for him. He passed out.

He remained in a half-drunken state for three days. The phone was kept off the hook and he didn't answer his door bell. He continued to drink until he passed out. He placed old newspapers on the rugs for Gino to use. He didn't have the energy to take the dog outside for his usual airings. Every now and then John would try to eat, but the food refused to stay down. If he didn't make it to the bathroom on time, he'd vomit anywhere he happened to be standing. Surrounded by his expensive furniture, in an apartment with a beautiful view, John was left with nothing but dog shit and his own vomit. He didn't wash himself and was aware of a strong odor that came from his person. John no longer cared. He wanted very much to die.

***

Edith and Bill were finally relaxed. Three days had passed and John hadn't bothered them. They were both beginning to feel that that particular nightmare might be over. Bill was even thinking about returning to his own apartment. When he mentioned it to Edith, she didn't object. She felt they were together, no matter where he lived. As Edith picked up her *New York Times* from outside the door, an article on the first page caught her eye. She quickly returned to bed to read all the details.

"Listen to this," she said.

Bill looked at her as he sipped his coffee.

"John's under indictment. He's being accused by the SEC of making phony land deals. God, it's hard to believe."

"Why?" said Bill. "Did you already forget that he was walking around toting a gun and threatening to kill someone with it?"

Edith didn't respond. She was thinking about John and knew this humiliation might be the end of him. She felt a twinge of compassion for him. She had never thought of John as being dishonest and yet wondered what options he had in the world of big business. The rules were set. One either played the game or got out. Edith knew that money was the most important thing in John's life, so in all likelihood the charges against him were true. She also knew he'd gone crazy and wouldn't know how to cope with the situation rationally. She sipped her coffee, lit a cigarette, and put down the paper.

"I bet he blows his brains out."

Bill shrugged his shoulders indifferently. "Better his than mine."

That afternoon Bill packed the few belongings he'd brought with him and kissed Edith good-bye. They both felt safe and relieved. Edith was tired. The tension was gone and exhaustion had taken over. She wanted to sleep.

"I'll be over in a day or two. Give yourself some time alone to relax. Everyone needs it."

Edith knew he was right and looked forward to a few days to herself.

John wanted to see Edith. He wanted to talk with her and hear her voice. At this point he'd nothing to lose so he picked up the phone and called her. He was more rational now than he had been in a long, long time. She answered the phone.

"I would like to see you."

Edith's answer was simple. "All right."

"Can I come to your apartment?"

Simplicity again.

"All right."

"I'll be there in half an hour."

John put down the receiver and went to wash his face. He stepped over all the filth that had accumulated, barely noticing it. John looked at his reflection in the bathroom mirror and didn't connect the defeated man that looked back at him with himself. He splashed cold water on his face and let it go at that. "Maybe I should take a shower," he thought, but then couldn't muster up the energy for one. In fact, he wondered if he had enough strength to change his clothes. He knew he could just about manage to get his body mobile enough to get to Edith's apartment. Doing any more than that was too much for him.

As he walked through the lobby of his building he never noticed the curious stares of the neighbors and doormen. He was concentrating very hard on getting to Edith. John no longer wanted to hurt her and didn't recall that he'd ever done anything more than want to get to her. One of the doormen got him a taxi. John didn't acknowledge him and closed the taxi door in his face. He remembered Edith's address but wasn't sure he remembered Edith.

Edith waited for John to arrive. She wasn't frightened of him any more. She knew by the pleading tone of his voice that he was no longer capable of hurting her. She felt he hadn't given her a choice. Her reaction seemed odd in light of his past threats and hideous phone calls. But she instinctively knew that his defeat had taken priority over his aggression. He was in enormous trouble and Edith realized what an emotional tightrope he walked. To have refused him would have been too cruel. But, just the same, Edith placed a sharp kitchen knife under one of the cushions on her couch.

The door bell rang and Edith let John in. She was immediately struck by his smell. After he was seated, Edith took a good look at him. He looked worse than a Bowery bum.

"Would you care for a drink, John?"

He nodded his head.

"A martini?"

He nodded his head again.

She wondered if he'd lost his tongue as well as his mind. As they sat sipping their drinks, Edith thought she might choke on the smell emanating from John's body. That they were once lovers seemed inconceivable. Edith was very sorry for him. She knew she was looking at a broken man and felt no particular power over him or smugness. All the people he had damaged paled in her mind. She realized that any victory of her own had nothing to do with his defeat. He'd always been defeated, but only now did she truly understand that. It forced her to wonder how she'd ever been able to be with such a broken man. I must have been broken myself, she thought.

John looked into his martini glass as he spoke.

"I don't know what to do."

Edith didn't respond and John continued.

"I can't do anything. I have no energy. It was hard for me to wash my face. My hair is oily. I remember you always hated oily hair. Remember, Edith?"

"Yes, I remember."

Actually she didn't know what discussion or incident concerning oily hair he was referring to, but thought it was best to "remember" if he wanted her to. He was so vulnerable at the moment that Edith knew her words could easily swing him one way or another. She knew she could torture him with criticism or indifference, but she wanted to be kind instead. She'd only hate herself if she attacked this pathetic man.

"I've been accused of being a thief."

"I know. I read it in the paper."

"It's all true. Every goddamn, fucking thing is true."

Edith wondered if he wanted her to reproach him. She said nothing. She had once wanted revenge for his coldness and now he sat before her in defeat. Revenge wasn't as sweet as the magic "they" said it was. Edith poured them each another drink and spoke.

"What are you going to do?"

"That's why I'm here. I want you to tell me."

Edith thought he sounded like a frightened child coming to his mother for help. She spoke to him firmly.

"I think you'd better muster up all your strength, get a good lawyer, and defend yourself as best you can. Your life is on the line and only you can fight for it."

John nodded his head and looked at Edith quizzically.

"What did you say?"

"It wasn't important, John."

He began to speak again. "You know, there's a part of me that wants to give up. The disgrace will ruin my career and defending myself will take all the money I have. I can't live without my money. I don't exist without my money."

Edith thought he was more lucid now than he had ever been before and pitied him. She knew he'd gone mad but he seemed more human than she'd ever seen him.

"I'm truly sad for you. That's all I can say."

"Do you want me to go?"

Edith felt a deep dread at what she knew she was going to say.

"I see no point in your staying."

John stood up.

"I guess my wish was for you to take me back. I need you very much."

Edith took his hand and walked him to the door.

"There's nothing I can do for you. I'm not your mother, wife, or girl friend. I'm just someone you knew once a long time ago."

Edith kissed him lightly on the cheek. His odor no longer bothered her. She opened the door. Without even looking at her, he left. His departure was a relief and Edith secretly prayed never to hear from him again.

She decided to write to Sarah and let her know about John. She wasn't sure if Sarah even read the newspapers at the Zen Center.

Sarah was happy to receive a letter from Edith.

She went to her small sparse room and sat down on her cot. She wanted to read her letter in privacy.

Dear Sarah,

I hope this letter finds you happy and well. Life has become very difficult in the Big Apple. You're lucky to be out West meditating. Sarah, John's gone crazy. He spent the last few weeks watching me, following me, and leaving notes at my door. More recently he returned to his old pattern of lewd phone calls. But all that is finished now. He was caught swindling funds from his publicly owned company and faces the possibility of going to jail. He came to see me today. I know that sounds weird, but I felt sorry for him. It's in all the papers. He's really been disgraced. I think he might kill himself. I didn't know if you'd read about it or not, and thought you might want to know. I guess I always knew he was obsessed, but right underneath his obsession is madness. It's sad and creepy at the same time.

How's your life going? Have meditation and open spaces changed anything? I hope so, if that's what you want . . .

Sarah picked her head up from Edith's letter and ran her fingers through her hair. She needed a shampoo. I still don't know what I want, she thought. I just had to get away. I wonder if I'm just taking a vacation. Her eyes returned to the letter.

> Neither Bill nor I have done much work lately. He's starting to get back into it. I hope to begin again soon. We've grown close. I'm not sure we understand each other but we do seem to know one another. We don't hide who we are. I love him.
>
> Have you heard from Paul or Nicholas? Are they still real to you now that you're so far away from home?

"Actually they aren't," thought Sarah, "and never were." She noticed as the days went by that both men receded more and more into the background of her life. She thought about John, the phone calls from him and the pain she had inflicted on Edith that day she'd played the tape for her. It made her wonder what her true feelings were toward her childhood friend. She didn't dwell on it for long, as she was anxious to return to the letter.

> I was rummaging through my closets the other day and found an old diary of yours. I don't know how it came into my possession. It dates back to high school. I began to read it, but stopped when I realized it wasn't mine. I'll send it to you soon.
>
> Well, that's about all for now. I just wanted you to know about John and get a reaction from you. It made me wonder about myself and my involvement with him. Maybe while you're meditating you

could think about it too. Write when you can.

Love,
Edith

Sarah put down the letter and lay down on the cot. She stared at the ceiling. She knew that today was her turn to sweep and mop the floors and it angered her. Sarah was waiting to be roshi's special darling. "I'll just have to be patient," she sighed. She wondered if she'd traveled clear across the country to become a maid. Edith's letter depressed her. Everything depressed her. Nothing ever turned out as she expected. She got up from her cot knowing it was getting late and her chores had to get done.

***

John returned to his apartment. He wondered why he felt so cold. His body would not stop shaking. He went into his bedroom and got under the covers, trying to warm himself. His legs quivered. He felt acute hunger pains and realized he was starved. He wished he could stop shaking long enough to get something to eat. His stomach felt empty. He held the covers close to his chin, turned on to his side and drew his legs up to his chest. He rocked his body back and forth, trying to stop the shaking.

"I must get to the kitchen . . . It's important that I eat. Oh God, I'm starving."

God. He'd never really thought about God. He'd never known the difference between right and wrong, so for him no God had existed. He suddenly began to silently pray.

"God, please take away the dampness from my bones and help me to find the strength to fill my empty stomach."

He kept the covers around him and tried to get out of bed. He fell back down. "Try again," he thought. With a sudden thrust, he pushed his body up again. It felt as if an electric shock had passed through him. His body stopped shaking and he walked into the kitchen. He dropped the covers on the living room floor. His hands quickly reached for something in the refrigerator. He opened his mouth and took a huge bite from an apple. Then he looked at it. It was covered with mold. "Goddamn it." Everything he pulled out of the refrigerator was rotten. He quickly pulled open all the cabinets in the kitchen, trying to find something to eat. He grabbed a box of potato chips and devoured them. "Thank God for junk food." Suddenly he began to shiver again.

"Where are those blankets? God, it's cold in here. I better get back to bed."

He picked the blankets up from the floor as he made his way back to the bedroom. He still felt hungry but everything was rotten. He wondered where his dog was and realized Gino hadn't been fed for days. His shaking body once more got out of bed. He walked into the living room, looking for Gino. He found him lying silently on the floor. He looked sick. John quickly brought him some dog food. "This can't be rotten," he thought. He watched Gino devour the food. His body was now going into spasms, but he managed to bring more food to his dog.

Soon he moved his body to the floor and found himself reaching for the dog food. The two of them sat together, dog and master, greedily eating from the same bowl. John scooped the food up with his hands and pushed it into his mouth. Bits of dog food crusted around his lips and his chin. John jealously noted that Gino's mouth moved fasther than John's hands. This made him want to go directly to the food as Gino did. He stretched his body out flat on his stomach and stuck his head in the bowl. He tried licking up the food with his tongue like the dog did. He wasn't very successful and attacked the food directly with his teeth. His face collided with Gino's face. Suddenly he felt a sharp pain. Gino had bit his chin.

He jerked his body up and touched his chin with his finger. It was bleeding. John couldn't believe it. His sweet, obedient dog wouldn't share his food with him, had even tried to hurt him. That ungrateful mutt, he thought. He's no better than the rest of them. He stood up, looked down at his dog, who was still eating, and spat at him. Then he returned to his bedroom.

He calmed down as he got back in his bed. He remembered the gun in his night table and took it out. He liked the feel of it. He looked at it and smiled. He was now completely calm and he knew his stomach would never be full. The gun moved back and forth in his hand.

"My whole problem was being in the wrong profession. I should have been a gangster."

John laughed. Something struck him funny.

"I really liked that dog food." He laughed again. "That was the best meal I've had in years." His laughter became almost hysterical.

He gripped the gun tighter, pointed it at his head, and proceeded to blow his brains out.

***

EXECUTIVE UNDER INVESTIGATION SHOOTS SELF

Edith wasn't surprised by the headline in the *Times*. She knew John was a man with few options. She wondered if she could have done more to help him. Her thoughts flashed back to their last meeting. To have taken him back would have meant sacrificing her own life for his. Edith was unnerved and went to see Bill.

She opened his apartment door with her own key and let herself in. Bill was in his den typing. Edith entered and placed the newspaper story on top of his typewriter. He stopped typing and read. Edith sat down on the couch and waited for his reaction. She moved her right index finger back and forth across her lips as she stared at Bill. The sun streamed through the room and warmed her face. Bill finished reading and looked up at Edith. She spoke.

"I feel terrible and somehow a little responsible."

She hadn't told Bill about John's visit with her because she knew he would never have understood. She also had felt it was something between John and her. Bill's face registered surprise.

"I can understand you being upset, but why do you feel responsible?"

"I don't know."

Bill thought a moment before responding.

"Thoughts don't kill, Edith. Maybe you wished him dead but according to the newspaper, he killed himself."

Edith self-consciously looked down at her feet when she answered him.

"John came to me the other day for help and I refused him. I tried to be kind and supportive, but he knew I didn't really care. Maybe I feel guilty because, up until the end, even knowing he was a beaten man, I still wanted to torture him. It makes me feel disgusted with myself."

If Bill was surprised by this news, he didn't show it.

"The point is, Edith, you didn't torture him. You did quite the reverse. By your own admission, you were kind. How long are you going to punish yourself for your thoughts?"

Edith looked up from her feet and stared directly

into Bill's eyes.

"I don't know."

She stayed with Bill for the remainder of the day. She didn't want to be alone because she felt frightened. Bill continued to work and Edith read a book. Little conversation passed between them, but it didn't matter. Edith was comforted by his presence. He seemed so sane and reliable. She stretched her body out on the couch and allowed the sun to warm her. Every now and then she'd glance over at Bill. Gradually she relaxed and the knot of tension in her stomach disappeared. She felt as if a shroud of darkness had covered her for her entire life and only now was lifting. She was content.

That night Edith and Bill made love as they never had before. They were moving into a new space together. No talk passed between them as they reached for each other's bodies. Words were not needed. To feel one another was what they both wanted. He moved his body up and down inside of her. Her insides burned and yearned for more, and they grabbed for it. He didn't stop until they reached their pinnacle together. Then, with a burst of release and joy, it was over. He moved his body onto his side and took her with him. His prick remained inside of her, and they fell asleep.

A few hours later Edith opened her eyes to the feel of Bill's hand caressing her breast.

"What are you thinking about?" she asked.

"Occasionally I dream of making love to three women at the same time." Bill was being both sexy and playful.

"Tell me about it," said Edith. She wanted to share everything he felt, thought, or fantasized. He continued to stroke her body as he spoke.

"One would be kissing my lips, another kissing my cock, and the last," he paused for a moment, "would be licking my toes."

"Licking your toes?"

For some reason that image struck Edith as funny and she began to laugh. Bill looked at her laughing. His voice was teasing when he spoke.

"Why don't you try it?"

"All right, I will."

Edith moved slowly to the end of the bed. She looked at Bill's feet and felt indifferent to them. Some people's feet repulsed her, that's why she'd never thought of them as sensual.

She began by licking one toe at a time. Instinctively she started with the smallest and moved to the largest. His toes suddenly became like his penis to her. She took each one in her mouth, caressed it with her tongue, kissed it with her lips, and gently bit it with her teeth. She moved up to his feet. Every part of him was beautiful because he allowed her to discover his body in her own way. There were no rules; nothing was forbidden: It was all there for her to discover. She didn't feel jealous of his fantasies. They helped her release her own.

She got on top of him and, this time, she made love to him. His hand stroked her breasts, her ass, her hair, as she moved on top of him. She looked down at his face and saw his excitement. This increased her own. He suddenly threw her over on her back and entered her. She knew he was ready to come. He moved deeper and deeper inside of her. Edith reached for his arms to anchor her. She was ready to receive all that was in him. He knew it and held nothing back. This time he stayed on top of her until they were both ready to sleep.

***

After receiving Edith's letter and hearing about John, Sarah made sure to read the newspaper each day. She was waiting for something about John to appear. Edith had said in her letter that she thought John might kill himself, but when she read that it actually had happened, she became deeply depressed. Since her mother's suicide, Sarah had felt doomed and refused to use her resources to fight what she thought would be her fate. Her recurring nightmare was that she would always be on the wrong side of things, never having what she wanted. Even roshi wasn't paying enough attention to her.

The fact that she had always participated in creating this situation was a notion which always eluded her. She'd rather blame it on the gods, or bad luck. These feelings returned when she read about John. She identified with him and felt he had also had bad luck. Sarah didn't feel like writing or speaking to Edith about it. She didn't feel Edith would be sympathetic enough.

The diary Edith had sent to her arrived that morning. She knew she must have been about seventeen years old when she wrote in it. Sarah wondered how it had come into Edith's possession. She also wondered if Edith had told her the truth when she said she hadn't read it. She leafed through the pages quickly. "I'll read it tonight," she thought. "No, I'd better read it now." Sarah sat down on the one chair in her room. The diary remained closed on her lap. For some reason she was afraid to read it, but her curiosity won out and she opened the secret book.

MARCH 31st

It has been a beautiful sunny day. Today's my first day of vacation. It feels so good. I just started WASHINGTON SQUARE by James. It seems good. Edith is here working on Hemingway. She does not understand why I keep a diary. I know why I do: I have to get my thoughts out somewhere. I have trouble expressing them verbally. Not that I express much. But it is as if I'm writing to a friend. I felt upset for a while when I was rereading my diary the other day. I was so unaware of what I'd done and said. It surprised me enormously. I have a nice relationship with Edith. She's really my best friend.

I'm going through a period of about a week where I have not been able to draw. I love to draw but sometimes I think I am kidding myself in thinking I can. Everything I have drawn up to now is but an attempt to express what I see. I have never been able to draw exactly what I see. That's one bad thing about my drawing: I draw or attempt to draw what I see but do not attempt to surpass my limited vision. It's dinner time. Of course I'm not hungry. Oh well. I must think about the people who are starving who would appreciate the food so much.

APRIL 1st

I should really get back to my reading but I have so much to say. You know I really loved HAMLET. I think it was my favorite Shakespeare play. It amazes me that Shakespeare had such total insight into people and their conflicts, appearance and reality, everything. He knew everything. WASHINGTON SQUARE is really good. I have so much work it almost angers me.

I feel kind of sad today, kind of alone. I'm also disappointed in myself for eating too much when I should lose a good ten pounds. It's upsetting to feel you're the fattest person on the street, in your home, next to Edith. And further into it, I'm very disappointed that I even care about it. My stomach's so bloated. My eyes feel so heavy but my mind is so damn awake. Mommy's so good-looking. It kills me. Why can't I see myself right? Edith's face is so beautiful. Sometimes I just feel like living alone, happy. I'm so tired, and Edith's coming in an hour. We're going to a Chinese restaurant for dinner. I hope it's nice.

I hope I don't get complexes. I always get insecure about my exterior. I worry about my legs being too long, about my freckles or pimples. It's so ridiculous. And I always wish I had bigger breasts. Always. Mine are so small. Not that it's important. None of it is, but for something so unimportant I sure waste time thinking about it. I'm scared of looking good. It scares me when I see how beautiful I can be, so I cover myself up in big long skirts which hide my body. It's so incredibly stupid. Meanwhile people die of hunger, get sacrificed, raped, die of diseases. My God . . . and I sit here like a spoiled brat crying over freckles and height. There is something radically wrong with me! Thank God I only go through these things periodically. Look away from yourself out into the world . . . there are so many things to discover.

APRIL 2nd

Right now I'm listening to some music on the radio. I never heard it before.It's great. Last night Edith and I went to a terrific restaurant. There were mirrors all over it so that you could constantly observe people without them noticing you. The waiter was nice too. He gave us extra fortune cookies. I really liked it there. We ate so much. Incredible. We talked about each other, about next year, about this summer. We both have so many of the same feelings. Today is a happy day.

April 3rd

I swear I hate myself. I eat and eat and am fatter than five thousand bulls. I hate mommy for being so skinny. I want to starve myself but I crave that cheese and cereal and everything that's in the kitchen and I'm not even hungry. Oh God I wish I could cut it out already. I really feel totally insane, totally. I'm a superficial fool. I'm a fat monster. How did this happen to me? And why? I have tons of pimples, my stomach's so damn bloated, and my ass is totally flabby. God, and I eat to make matters worse! Why? I hate it so much. I can't wait to get away from home and stop it already. I feel just awful and terribly ill at ease. I'm just dying to play tennis. Dying to. I'm sickening . . . What makes me even more sickening is that I think about it and care about it. STOP IT! You fool! I feel like crying.

***

Sarah gently closed her diary. She didn't want to read anymore and be reminded of her adolescent life and thoughts. She hid the diary in one of her drawers and lay down on her bed. She was tired and didn't feel like talking to anyone. She tried to sleep, but her irrational agonies from the past kept her awake. She wondered if she'd ever really conquered her complexes. It was crazy, she thought. Some people called her beautiful; she'd imagined herself ugly and grotesque. She wondered if she should call Edith the next day to say hello. She hoped Edith hadn't read her diary. Sarah knew her friend would find the journal steeped in self-pity and self-indulgence. A teenager's prerogative, she thought. Sarah once more hoped the changes she had made in her life would strengthen her. She knew they were long overdue. It was time to sleep. Sarah was very tired.

***

Bill and Edith sat quietly in Bill's double bed smoking cigarettes. They had just finished making love. A sheet covered their bodies. Bill appeared serious and Edith felt his lovemaking had been strained. After finishing one cigarette and lighting another, Bill turned to Edith and spoke.

"How would you like to live in California?"

"What for?" Edith's voice registered surprise.

"Well, my great American novel isn't turning out too great and I need money. I was offered a job writing a pilot for TV. If a network buys it, I can become the story editor. Looking at it realistically, I need the work."

Edith's whole body flooded with anxiety. She tried to be calm when she spoke.

"You know how much I hate California. I don't think I could write out there. To leave New York now seems wrong."

Bill appeared not to have heard her.

"We'd live together, or if you wanted we could marry."

Edith was truly moved and found herself speechless. Bill looked at her and saw the tears moving down her cheeks. He took her hand and said nothing.

Edith felt him withdraw more and more into himself. She found it very difficult to be with him and to feel him so removed from her. After they had sat together for a while in almost utter silence, she had to say something.

"You've become totally aloof. It's just plain selfish at a time like this."

Bill seemed surprised by her outburst, as though he hadn't even been aware of his withdrawal. He spoke apologetically.

"I'm really sorry, Edith. You should always tell me when I get this way. I'm used to withdrawing when I'm worried or hurt. It's something I have to fight. Half the time I'm not even conscious of it."

He was being so contrite that Edith felt a twinge of guilt for having brought the subject up. But, in thinking about it, she knew they were both relieved that she had. "Our relationship might have been permanently weakened if I'd said nothing," she thought. In truth, Bill welcomed Edith's help in trying to break a pattern of behavior that by now had become automatic with him. He tightened his grip on her hand.

"I love you," he said.

Edith removed her hand from his and held him in her arms. Nothing was black or white any more for Edith. Life had become complicated.

***

Edith was having trouble writing. She had grown listless. Separations in every direction now seemed imminent for her. Sarah was gone and they communicated less and less frequently. Now Bill was speaking of leaving. Edith rested her elbows on her typewriter and put her head in her hands. She was thinking about moving to California.

She hated the life-style there. The fact that the seasons never changed and no cultural stimulation existed bothered her. The thought of living in a car, of having to drive everywhere, was depressing, but most of all she couldn't bear to leave the throngs of people that she saw every day on the streets of New York.

"He wants me to marry him but right now California feels so wrong."

She listened to the sound of her voice and shook her head.

"No, it's just wrong."

She became quiet and stared into space. She rationalized her fear of Bill leaving by thinking that, if she and Bill were going to settle into a permanent relationship, the time apart wouldn't alter that. They could write, speak on the telephone, and take turns visiting one another. "We'd have two lives instead of one," she thought.

Edith could not predict how she would feel without Bill in her life. She knew that she loved him, but felt she'd have to try going it alone for a while. "California is too bleak. I can always change my mind. If I lose him then he isn't worth the commitment." These were her rationales and helped to alleviate some of her pain.

Since that night neither she nor Bill had talked about his move again. She knew he was allowing her time to reach her decision. Whatever it was, she knew he'd understand. Of that Edith was certain. When they spoke on the phone, both of them tried to be natural. It was difficult because neither he nor she was saying what was uppermost in their thoughts.

Edith couldn't quite believe Bill would actually be leaving her. The panic which might set in once he was really gone scared her more than whatever present decision she'd now have to make. She felt some hideous punishment might await her if she let Bill leave without her. It was irrational, but just the same real. Edith wondered if she might crumble, or was she really afraid that Bill would be the one to come apart. These thoughts left her paralyzed, unable to make a decision, afraid to admit to Bill that she didn't want to leave New York.

She lit a cigarette and looked down at the empty sheet of paper in her typewriter. She wondered if she had some strange religion which filled her with fear at the prospect of doing what she thought best for herself. Fear was beginning to bore her and she suspected this might be the moment to change her religion. She decided it was time to say what she felt. Thought she knew she'd always been honest with Bill in the past, she was afraid to say no to his offer now. If the sky didn't fall and she wasn't struck by lightening, maybe she'd feel less frightened.

Edith sighed and went on thinking. Her cigarette had burned out in the ash tray and she hadn't even smoked it. At all cost she knew she must not permit herself to feel like a small child standing helpless in the corner. Edith decided to speak with Bill immediately. She wanted to express her irrational sense of feeling betrayed. "If he loves me, he'll find a way to stay," she thought. Edith had to tell him and risk exposing her bratty side. She knew it was the only way they could remain in love.

Edith invited Bill for dinner. She knew there would be a confrontation. The tension of not knowing exactly what she was going to say gave her the urge to urinate. She went to the bathroom but found herself unable to go. It wouldn't come. Something held it back as if she was afraid of being heard. As she sat on the toilet she remembered how she had been as a little girl in public rest rooms. She remembered how she had prayed to God to help her to urinate if other people were outside waiting for her toilet. To this day, Edith put on the water if someone was able to hear her in the bathroom. She wondered once more about this religion or God of hers that could help her to urinate in public rest rooms but might punish her with a vengeance if she said or did as she pleased.

Edith took great pains in getting dressed for the evening. Most of the time she didn't fuss a great deal when she saw Bill, but tonight she wanted to look particularly good. Edith bathed for what seemed like an excessive period of time and then dabbed on some French rose water. She put on more makeup than usual. She moved with a sense of anticipation. After deciding against two or three dresses, she finally chose a green cotton knit that plunged slightly at the neckline and had a slit on either side of the hem. The only accessory that she wore was a large ivory bracelet. The last thing she put on were high-heeled lizard sandals which she never wore because the heels were so high she couldn't walk in them for more than twenty minutes. Edith knew Bill would probably be wearing his dungarees and that she'd most certainly overdressed for the occasion, but she didn't care. She looked at her reflection in the mirror, studying herself carefully, pulling on separate strands of her hair to make them perfect. She finally felt satisfied.

Bill arrived promptly at seven. He looked surprised as he stepped into Edith's apartment.

"You look great," he said, as he handed her two bottles of wine.

He was wearing his dungarees but he had also put on a nice shirt and classic corduroy jacket. Though his attire was quite conventional, Edith always thought this sort of rig-out made men look as though they were two separate people. But it pleased Edith that Bill wasn't the type of man who gave too much thought to his clothes. Edith was nervous and immediately went to the kitchen to open the wine, grateful to be doing something with her hands. Bill walked up behind her and put his arms around her waist. He squeezed her in a way that tickled. Edith giggled and gave him a friendly push away.

"You really do look great, Edith. I love your dress, it matches your eyes. Let me help you open the wine."

She handed him the Soave Bolla and returned to the livingroom with glasses in hand. When Bill walked toward her with the wine, she was struck by his thick head of blond hair and twinkling blue eyes. It made her happy to see him walk across the room. There was a quality of *politesse* about him which never ceased to warm her heart. They sat down to drink their wine and Edith looked at Bill out of the corner of her eye. She caught him staring at her. He was waiting for her to speak. She obliged.

"What I have to say I know is irrational, unreasonable, and selfish. It has nothing to do with reality. But the truth is, I'm in a rage."

Bill listened to her. Edith thought she saw a trace of a smile cross his lips.

"Do you always get so dressed up when you're in a rage?"

Edith threw him an impatient glance and continued with her speech.

"I keep thinking that if you really loved me, you'd find a way to stay in New York. Sometimes I get so paranoid, I'm sure you asked for the job."

Bill's voice was calm, but it had a touch of impatience in it.

"If I was trying to get rid of you, would I have asked you to come with me?"

"I said I was being irrational."

"Well, stop having a tantrum and give me an answer, preferably one that makes sense." Bill took a large sip of his wine.

"I can't go. I'm terrified of being without you but feel my home is here for now. Maybe you'll be gone for a week and I'll realize I've made a terrible mistake. If that happens I hope you leave me the option to pack my bags and come to you. I love you, Bill."

"But not enough to move across the country with me."

Edith smiled—"Now who's having the tantrum?"

Bill stood up and paced the room.

"You're right, California stinks. I'd be busy every day and you'd be writing in an atmosphere that you didn't like."

Edith finished her drink and put down her glass.

"I couldn't have said it better myself."

"Well, dear lady, I want you to know that if you ever change your mind, I'll always want you."

Edith knew she was truly loved and felt a deep appreciation.

"I'll come visit the moment you're settled."

Bill looked at her. He was still standing, but no

longer pacing.

"I'd like that."

They both agreed that there was nothing more to be said on the subject, and sat down to a pleasant dinner. That night Edith and Bill made love. She cried the whole time. She couldn't remember ever having felt so sad. Yet, despite her tears, she was able to give herself completely because she knew Bill loved her. In time, they fell asleep in each other's arms.

Bill was expected in California in a week. Edith had moved in with him for the remaining time. The days dragged by. Bill's apartment was filled with half-packed suitcases, books being prepared for shipment, and empty walls where pictures had once hung. Edith recalled that Sarah's room at the Chelsea had looked much the same. She wondered if she was making a mistake by not going. The days felt as though they would never end. Edith tried to write while Bill packed and prepared himself for his move. They were together in Bill's den. Each time Edith looked up from her typewriter, she'd catch Bill's eyes wandering from his work.

Finally they both gave up. Bill walked to the window and looked out at the city. He seemed to be noticing it for the first time.

"I love this city. It's my home," he said.

"I know. It's so human. We take it for granted."

Bill looked away from the window and into

Edith's face.

"Let's go for a walk."

Edith smiled and stood up.

They walked hand in hand through the city streets. There was something reassuring about so many other people doing the same thing. Neither of them spoke. There was too much to say and no one place to begin. They understood each other's silence. Edith could tell by the set of Bill's body that he was trying to conceal the great tension he felt about leaving. She couldn't help him, for she was doing the same. They stopped to look at paintings on display in a gallery window. They were Morandi still lifes. "They look so lonely," thought Edith.

Edith and Bill found themselves wandering through SoHo. The shops and galleries which had always caught their attention in the past held little interest for them today. Edith finally stopped to look in the window of one shop that sold only white Edwardian lace underwear. Edith had often passed it alone. She looked at Bill and smiled.

"These clothes always arouse me."

Bill stood staring at the window.

"Did they conjure up great fantasies in that mind of yours?"

"Uh-huh."

"Well, don't you think you should share them with me?" Bill said teasingly.

Edith dropped his hand and put her arms

through his. She spoke softly into his ear.

"I'd imagine myself in bed wearing one of these lacy nightgowns and waiting for my lover. Sometimes I decided I'd finish with one man in the afternoon, wearing black satin, and after he left I would change into one of these Edwardian whites to wait for my second lover of the day. That fantasy stopped when I met you."

"That doesn't seem fair," said Bill. He pulled her by the arm to the door and they entered the store.

"Tonight you wear black satin *and* white lace."

Bill bought the two negligees that were displayed in the window. Then they continued on their walk, aware of each other's bodies and anticipating the night together.

Edith slipped on her new black nightgown. It had a plunging neckline. The fabric clung to her body, completely exposing it. Bill watched her as she got into bed next to him. She looked at him and saw that he was wearing pajamas. He'd never worn them before. She began to laugh, and laugh and laugh. He looked at her and also broke into laughter. It was a sudden release of tension for the both of them. The tears were waiting to spring forth right beneath their hysterical laughter.

"I'll take my pajamas off if you take your nightgown off."

"It's a deal."

In a moment they were both naked. Bill

immediately entered her.

"This is much nicer, isn't it?"

Edith didn't answer him. She only wanted to reach an orgasm and have him do the same. He was leaving her soon and she wondered if she could ever get enough of him.

Edith was the one remaining home, yet she was the one who felt homesick. When she'd walk into the bedroom, the sound of Bill's small portable clock ticking on the night table stirred a yearning within her. The plant that sat on the windowsill made her eyes fill up. She never wanted to leave Bill's side. He hadn't left her yet and she already missed him.

Bill felt her clinging to him, and understood. He didn't think her dependency was only because of their imminent separation. Bill recognized that Edith was taking the more difficult road by not going with him. He respected her for it. She had made her decision on the basis of what she thought was best for herself. Bill knew she wanted to try going it alone for a while. He wasn't sure if Edith was aware of that fact, but he imagined she probably was. He thought her uncharacteristic need to be with him at all times was because she was holding on to some small part of herself that still remained a little girl. Once he was gone, he suspected she would take the time to really grow and blossom as a woman. It might take a long time, he mused. But he loved her and was willing to wait.

***

Sarah called Edith to say hello. Edith informed her of Bill's departure.

"He's leaving tomorrow. He got a good job offer and decided to take it."

Sarah was surprised by this news and wondered how her friend really felt.

"You must feel deserted with everyone leaving."

"At this point I'm numb," Edith answered her playfully. "You, Bill, it seems like everyone I love is abandoning me."

"Why don't you come out here too?"

"I can't right now."

Sarah didn't press her for reasons.

"You'll always have a place to visit and it should be interesting to see how you make out."

"I'll be all right." Edith paused for a moment before speaking again. "Did you receive the diary yet? I still can't figure out how it found its way into my apartment."

"Yes, I got it the other day. It depressed me. I threw it out."

Edith became uncomfortable and wanted to get off the phone. She once again had the feeling that Sarah was blaming her for something.

"Bill will give you a call when he gets there.

He'd love to see someone from home."

"What flight is he taking? I can pick him up at the airport."

Edith reluctantly gave Sarah the information.

"Any chance of you returning to New York, Sarah?"

"I don't think so. I'm determined to stick to something in my life."

"I know what you mean."

There was a thick silence between them. Edith was sorry Sarah had called her. She realized that neither of them had mentioned John's death and knew it would always come between them.

"Tell Bill I'll see him tomorrow and write or call if you get lonely."

"Thanks. Take care."

Edith hung up the telephone with the knowledge that she and Sarah were no longer friends. She felt uneasy knowing Sarah would be with Bill and realized she didn't trust her. The more she dwelled on it, the more convinced she was that Sarah might try, in some subtle way, to seduce him. She decided not to discuss her doubts with Bill. She knew she trusted him and for the moment that was all that mattered to her. Again she wondered if she was making a mistake by not going. No point rehashing it, she thought. She'd made her decision and intended sticking to it.

"Nothing is forever. Thank God for my writing." Edith knew it was the one constant in her life and nobody could take it away from her. She wished Bill would leave quickly. The anticipation was torture. Her life without him would require an adjustment but one Edith was preparing herself to make. The important thing for her was that she loved him, which meant that she was capable of loving. This thought helped alleviate some of her fear and sadness.

Bill was leaving the next morning. The two of them had already tasted the feelings of separation. That night they wanted to feel one another deeply inside. It helped restore life in them. When their bodies came together they knew they still had each other. Edith was overflowing with love and wanted only to give pleasure. Bill's hand felt so tender upon her body that she knew he really loved her. Her fingers responded, touching every inch of him. He felt so warm, so sturdy. It made Edith happy to feel secure and enraptured at the same time.

There was a new urgency between them that took the form of passion. She wasn't afraid. He could have been leading her to the moon and she would have followed him.

Suddenly Bill spoke. "I'd like you to take me in your mouth. I want you to swallow my come."

"Yes, yes," she said, and her mouth immediately opened. Her lips parted to welcome him. She made love to his prick with her tongue. She licked him with gentleness, trying to convey the tenderness she felt. His prick grew larger and larger. Her mouth was filled with him. His excitement thrilled her. When he came, she drank his come and, sublimely exhausted, they lay very still.

"Do you think you'll ever come to me, Edith?"

"Yes."

Nothing more was said. It was time to sleep.

The day finally arrived. Edith went with Bill to the airport. She watched him board the plane for California. Then she took a taxi home, thought about the book she was writing, and took a long, hot bath.